"*The Protector* delivers engaging characters, a fast-moving plot, and some very steamy love scenes. NL Gassert has crafted an exciting and entertaining romance that builds suspense and erotic tension with every turn of the page. Take it to bed...and plan on staying up."
Charles Casillo, author of *The Fame Game*

"Sexy, sizzling—and sweet! NL Gassert manages to combine the tenderness of first love with thrilling action in *The Protector*. The tropical setting on Guam is fresh and beautifully evoked, and the engaging characters of Mason and Soren will keep readers turning the pages, rooting for these lovers against tropical storms and terrorist agents."
Neil Plakcy, author of *Mahu Surfer*

"Literary chef Gassert serves up a delectable nine-course meal of murder, mayhem, money-laundering, terrorism, temptation, brutality, bisexuality, scandal, and sadistical (sic.) father-son abuse."
William Maltese, author of the Stud Draqual mystery series

"Gassert delivers taut action and intriguing characters in a lush, exotic setting that really sets this book apart—a promising debut!"
MJ Pearson, author of *Discreet Young Gentleman*

The Protector

by NL Gassert

Seventh Window
Publications

The Protector © 2008 NL Gassert

All rights reserved. Except for brief passages quoted in a newspaper, magazine, radio, or television review, no part of this book may be reproduced in any form or by any means, electronic or mechanical, including photocopying and recording, or by any information retrieval system, without permission in writing from the publisher.

This novel is entirely a work of fiction. Though it contains incidental references to actual people, products and places, these references are merely to lend the fiction a realistic setting. All other names, characters, places and incidents are the product of the author's imagination. Any resemblance to actual persons, living or dead, events or locales is entirely coincidental.

First Seventh Window Publications edition: January 2008
cover illustration © 2007 Aman Chaudhary – all rights reserved

Published in the United States of America by:
Seventh Window Publications
P.O. BOX 603165
Providence, RI 02906-0165

http://www.SeventhWindow.com

Library of Congress Control Number: 2007940879

ISBN-13:   978-0-9717089-6-9
ISBN-10:   0-9717089-6-7

dedication

In memory of Loren Black

acknowledgments

With thanks to Josh Aterovis, Deborah Turrell Atkinson, Lori L. Lake, and MJ Pearson for answering my questions about the publishing business and offering sage advice.

Many thanks also to Ken Harrison for understanding what I meant to write and making me actually write it. I will have more details and less hair color the next time around, I promise.

A heartfelt thank you to Ella, Laurie, Loren, Nigel, Reshenna and Tru for your support, encouragement and input. You guys rock!

1

The air over the marina was thick with September humidity. Moored to the dock, boats gently swayed as moonlit waves slapped up against their hulls. The scent of the Pacific Ocean saturated the night.

Mason Ward smiled to himself. But while the scene was idyllic, the situation was far from it. For one thing, the redhead walking down the dock beside him wasn't a date, and he wasn't walking as much as he was dragging his feet. Mason didn't date much, had in fact not been on a date in months, but men weren't usually this reluctant to share his company.

Of course, he had a lousy track record where redheads

were concerned. Right out of high school and still very much in denial about his attraction to men, he'd married a lovely and fire-headed girl. Today, Angela, his ex-wife of ten years, was as disinterested in him as the young man walking down the dock next to him. Mason couldn't help but wonder what he'd gotten himself into.

Not two hours before, past a time when polite people decided it was too late to call anyone in the same time zone, Mason's phone had rung. Although determined not to answer it, he'd still checked the display. It was Kaoru. His friend Kaoru called him infrequently enough that this late night call had aroused Mason's curiosity. He'd answered, and in typical fashion, Kaoru—only the second FBI agent to be born and raised on Guam—had skipped the small talk to come right to the point. "Listen, Mason, old buddy, I've got this kid who's in trouble. I need a safe place to stash him for a week or two."

Mason groaned, seeing his weekend plans grinding to a halt. "Are you looking for a babysitter or a bodyguard?"

"Both. The kid's knee-deep in some serious shit. But I'm having issues with his story. I need him somewhere safe and out of reach."

"How out of reach?"

"Extended cruise out of reach. I need him sober and away from his father."

"This father, is he a problem?"

"Yes," Kaoru said. "I'm going out on a limb here for the kid. I need someone I can trust to take him off my hands for a while, someone who can handle him and, if worse comes to worst, the father."

The call itself told Mason all he needed to know. His friend wasn't in the habit of looking for help outside the department.

"You won't regret it," Kaoru promised before he hung up.

Oh yes, I will, Mason thought. He had a feeling that bringing Soren Buchanan, James "The Smile" Buchanan's son, home with him had trouble written all over it.

Mason and Soren reached their destination at the end of the

long dock and Mason shot the sullen shadow to his right a very deliberate, very slow look, letting his eyes travel down Soren's lean frame. A few months shy of twenty-three. Just under six feet. Rangy. Hair like burnished copper. Eyes like jade. Cheekbone and jaw discolored with bruises. T-shirt stained with his own blood.

The kid shoved his hands into the front pockets of his faded Levis and stared at the dark yacht before them. "What's this?"

"A boat."

"I can see that."

Mason arched a dark brow and shrugged. The FBI's notes on Soren suggested that challenging authority came as naturally to him as breathing. And drinking. "Your home for the next two weeks."

"You've got to be kidding."

"I've been hired to keep you sober and out of your father's long reach. This will be it for the next two weeks."

The boat—a 58-foot Alaskan-style trawler—was a good idea. Not exactly Mason's first choice, because it was his home, but a good idea nonetheless. Still, the kid didn't seem inclined to board the yacht voluntarily. Mason gave him a firm nudge onboard when glaring at him didn't do the trick.

"Let me show you something." Mason maneuvered his guest into the pilothouse. He pointed to a navigational chart unrolled on the table. "We'll be here." He tapped the vastness of the Pacific Ocean with a manicured finger. "This is us right now." He swept his finger to the eastern edge of the chart where Guam's coastline was visible, making his point. He let that sink in.

"Now," he fixed the redhead with a measuring look, "let's get some things straight. There is no alcohol on board. None. And I'm a very thorough guy."

Soren shoved his hands back into the pockets of his jeans and tore his attention off the chart. "What does that mean?"

"That means," Mason explained, "I even threw out the mouthwash and the rubbing alcohol under the sink. You get into any scrapes, we've got peroxide."

"Screw you."

Mason grunted. On an island populated with tawny-skinned, dark-haired beauties, Soren was an exotic exception that drew the eyes of men and women alike. Mason's weakness for redheads aside, he wondered just how Soren would react to a come-on. Did Soren follow through or was he just a tease?

Mason grabbed him by the sleeve of his T-shirt, determined not to fall into the kid's trap. He led the redhead down two sets of stairs and a narrow passageway, into a large stateroom where Soren shook off his hand and turned to face him with narrowed green eyes that radiated disdain.

Mason straightened and crossed muscular arms in front of his chest. "Take your clothes off."

"What?"

Mason enjoyed the moment. Ruffling the kid's feathers wasn't easy, but it was certainly satisfying. "Your clothes," he repeated. "Take them off. I want to look at"—he gestured, not sure what to call the result of abuse—"you."

Soren ignored him, turning his back. He chose to inspect the spacious stateroom instead. His curious glance swept over gleaming teak and the dark sheets and blankets on the large, neatly made bed that dominated the room. He looked at books organized on shelves. Touched fingers to framed photographs grouped together between two open ports that let in the humid night air. Eyed the alphabetized CD collection. "This is nice."

"Yes, it is. Thank you. Don't get used to it. It's my bedroom. Yours is down there. Less nice." Mason pointed absently, sat on his bed and spread out the contents of his first-aid kit before him. There was the usual: adhesive bandages of all sizes, gauzes and such, and a few things he'd added over the years. Like Ben's homemade and pungent cure for rashes of all kinds. And his grandmother's ointment that soothed most aches and pains.

"Strip. Sit," he said, pointing at the edge of the bed.

Soren wrinkled his nose. "What's that smell?"

"Menthol."

He didn't move. Mason waited, stared. It was a short standoff. The kid caved in first. Mason heard Soren's muffled wince that accompanied the shirt sliding past red hair and saw the color drain from already pale skin.

Soren tossed the shirt to the side. It slid over the edge of the bed and onto the floor. He obviously didn't give it a second's thought, but Mason's fingers itched to pick it up. Instead, he waited until his guest sat gingerly on the bed, then moved behind him.

Someone had indeed been very pissed off, and from the looks of it Soren's back had suffered the brunt of the aggression, probably having been slammed up against a few hard surfaces. Mason suspected the kid was either still drunk or high on painkillers. Probably both. All the same, Soren hissed, cringed and flinched away from Mason's gentle touch and the cool salve he spread across the bruises and scrapes.

"So, who did this to you?"

Soren closed his eyes. He hung his head and his tousled hair—a tad too long for Mason's taste—fell to hide his face. "What do you care?"

His father, James "The Smile" Buchanan, was an active player on the political court. Despite four marriages, their failures and his appetite for vastly younger women, Buchanan could have been governor twice over. His whirlwind marriage to Soren's mother, a Swedish supermodel—a relationship whispered to have been a publicity stunt—had catapulted him out of the realm of politics and into full-fledged celebrity status. His list of wealthy and influential friends and acquaintances read like the Who's Who? of Guam.

But there was more to James Buchanan than his public persona. He wasn't a man to cross. He was too influential, too well connected, and, if rumors were true, too ruthless. Mason had the feeling that talk of a short fuse and a bad temper wasn't just idle gossip, not with the man's battered and bruised son sitting before him.

He watched the kid's shoulders tense as he ran a salved and slippery hand down Soren's bruised flank. Soren had the porcelain complexion of a natural redhead. The touch of bronze the constant and unrelenting Guamanian sun had added was barely enough to produce a tan line. It was quite a shame that the freckled skin was marred with bruises.

"So, Kaoru said your father did this to you. That true?"

"Do you always ask so many questions?"

"I get paid to ask questions."

"Ah."

"So, is it true?"

"Yes."

"Why?"

Soren sighed, shrugged, and winced. "I wasn't a model son. I embarrassed him in front of his business associates."

Mason made a low noise in the back of his throat. James "The Smile" Buchanan had a temper. Even Kaoru suspected violent opposition or he wouldn't have suggested taking the kid off the island. "Did you embarrass him?"

"I was drunk."

"You're drunk a lot." It was in the notes he'd read.

Soren's eyes snapped open and his head came up. He held Mason's even stare with a fierce look of his own. "No, I'm not."

"Uh huh."

"I am not." He jerked back when Mason examined a large bruise covering his ribs. "I'm not," he said again. "I don't drink all the time. Matter of fact, I don't drink all that often." He glared and sucked in a startled breath when Mason touched the bruise. "But when I do, I'm serious about it. I drink to get drunk. Shit. That hurts." He clamped his mouth shut and grimaced.

"I see." Mason's unsympathetic hand prodded the bruise again. "I don't think it's cracked. Take a deep breath."

"Why?"

"Just do it."

Soren pursed his lips and took a breath.

Mason sat back and fixed him with a look that would have had another man sucking more air into his lungs. "The idea is for you to move that rib when you breathe."

Soren did and grimaced again. "He waited until the next

day. My father. Waited till I was sober. Even gave me an aspirin for the hangover. Then he beat the shit out of me."

"Considerate."

"Yeah. You were kidding about the boat and the two weeks, right?"

"No."

"Shit. What if I get sea sick?"

"Do you?"

"I just might. You know, apparently being a recovering alcoholic and all."

"Wiseass." Oh yeah, he'd invited trouble onboard for sure. Trouble that had nothing to do with Soren being The Smile's son and everything to do with him sitting on Mason's bed, half naked, vulnerable, red hair tousled. He was a temptation, and Mason's dormant hormones—jarred awake by hands sliding over warm flesh—were begging for a taste. There was such a thing as professionalism, though. Hormones notwithstanding, Mason knew he'd reached the line that separated medicinal touch from caress. Reluctantly he took his hands off the kid.

"I don't have any clothes."

Mason nodded toward his dresser. "You can borrow some of mine."

Mason felt Soren's appraising glance slide over his body like a warm touch. He groaned and got to his feet, bringing distance between the tease and his willpower.

"I doubt they fit."

Mason took his own lingering look. "Feel free to strut around naked."

Soren pulled his split lips into a grin. "You wish."

"Less nice, my ass," Soren grumbled the next morning. When he'd thought his cabin would be a smaller version of Mason's bedroom, he'd been sorely mistaken. His 5-foot by 8-foot space came with an upper and a lower single bunk and just enough room for a man to take a deep breath.

Soren stumbled out of his cabin and up the few stairs. The man who stood in the galley, forking breakfast eggs and rice into his mouth when Soren shuffled past wasn't Mason. He was shorter and less broad across the shoulders. His dark hair and beard were shot through with silver. Glasses perched on his nose.

"Good morning," the man said. "Soren? Right?"

"Yeah." Soren squinted past sleep-tousled hair that fell onto his face and rubbed his throbbing temple. He heaved himself onto one of the stools in front of the galley counter, his back to the salon and the oversized couch he wanted to stretch out on, dropped his elbows onto the counter and his head into his hands. "Who are you?"

"Ben Marques. Mason's business partner."

Soren took one look at the forty-something Spaniard and pegged him for a silent partner, definitely not a bodyguard. His skepticism must have showed, because Ben smiled.

"I'm the office manager," he explained. "Want some breakfast?"

"Got a soda?"

"For breakfast? No. Sorry. No sodas." He laughed and held up his hands when Soren lifted his head and glowered at him. "No, what I meant to say was no sodas period. Mason doesn't believe in soda."

Soren made a face and jerked his chin in the direction of the large stainless steel fridge. He needed something to wash the sour taste off his tongue and jumpstart his sore body. "What's in there then?"

Ben abandoned his breakfast plate and stuck his dark head in the fridge to report his findings, "Milk. Water. Tomato juice."

Tomato juice? The thought alone made Soren's stomach churn and his bile rise. He gagged and for a split second considered downing half a glass. Throwing up might make him feel better. Little else would. "Where's the warden anyway?"

Ben chuckled. "In the shower. Want me to hunt down some aspirin for you?"

"Coffee?"

Ben grimaced. "Sorry, kid. No coffee either."

"No coffee? You're kidding, right? The man doesn't drink coffee?"

Ben shook his head.

"No soda. No coffee. What the hell?" Soren yanked a hand through his bed hair and eyed the long galley counter. Sure enough, there wasn't a coffee maker visible. What he did see when he let his gaze linger, and he had an eye for that, was the skilled craftsmanship that had gone into the joinery and cabinetry in the galley. Nice boat, he admitted reluctantly, then shook his head to clear it of the distraction.

"Well, what about me?" he whined. "I drink coffee." He narrowed his eyes at Ben. "What does he drink? Milk?"

"Tea, Mason drinks tea. But he's very particular about it. Between us," Ben lowered his voice and leaned in closer across the counter, "it needs sugar, lots of sugar, just don't let him see you put it in."

Soren groaned. He wasn't sure what he'd expected when he'd fled his father's house and turned to the FBI for protection. He'd been prepared for a no-nonsense motel/hotel, a duo of disinterested law enforcers, and take-out Chinese food; he watched TV after all. He hadn't expected Mason. Tall, dark and built like The Rock. About as unforgiving and unimpressionable as a freaking rock, too. With a fifty-somefoot boat. And a very gentle touch that sent pleasant shivers down Soren's spine. "I'm stuck with a freak. Jesus, he's not a vegetarian, is he? There's no way I can deal with vegetables for two weeks."

"There're a couple of steaks in the freezer," Mason said, and Soren all but jumped off his stool. "I hope you like fish. You'll be eating a lot of it."

His heart hammering against sore ribs, Soren rolled his eyes. "Probably have to catch it myself," he grumbled and shot Mason a dark look from under long lashes.

Freshly showered and shaven, in casual shorts and nothing else, Mason strolled around the long galley counter and dropped his large hand on Soren's shoulder. "Damn straight. This is no vacation. You'll have to work to earn your keep."

"I don't have to do shit."

Mason and Ben exchanged looks.

"I'm not doing your laundry," Mason said evenly as he crossed muscular arms over an equally impressive chest.

"What laundry?" Soren's memory was a little hazy, but he did remember packing a backpack before climbing out his bedroom window and turning to the FBI for help. Not that an extra T-shirt and a change of underwear would get him very far, which was partly why he sat here in the same clothes he'd worn the day before, which he'd worn the night before, which he'd pulled on after his father had finished with him and before he'd gotten drunk again.

"And if you plan on eating, then you better include cooking and dishes in those plans, too."

"You want me to do chores? I don't do chores."

"Tea?" Mason asked.

"What?"

"Do you want some tea?"

Ben was gesturing and shaking his head behind Mason's broad back, but Soren wasn't smart enough to take the advice. Or was it a warning? "Sure, I guess."

"Now, let's get some things straight. I'm not a U.S. Marshal, and I'm not with the FBI. So don't get any ideas about me having to follow any kind of official rules."

Soren made a face. Hulking Mason might be nicer to look at than the average law enforcer and his boat was a hell of a lot nicer than the average motel/hotel, but right now all Soren wanted was the kind of protective custody TV shows portrayed, with unlimited minibar privileges and take-out breakfast. And protectors that were easily manipulated.

"Kaoru is paying me to keep you out of trouble just long enough for him to decide what to do with you. He wasn't specific about how I was going to do that as long as it involved taking you on a fishing trip. So you can spend the next two weeks in your cabin or you can pitch in around here."

"Pitch in?" Soren glanced at Ben for help, but the man just shook his head. Was he coming on this trip, too? "Never mind. Listen, I appreciate the help, really, I do, but this isn't going to work out. I should … go."

Mason put the tea kettle on the stove. "Go?"

"Yes, go. Like somewhere else." Where they had coffee and soda, where he wasn't required to wash his own clothes or fish for his dinner. "You're … we're … I didn't know what the hell I was doing … I can take care of myself."

"Yeah, I can see that." Mason reached across the counter, took Soren's chin in hand and tipped his bruised face to the side. "Ben can see that, too."

Ben nodded.

At six foot four and over two hundred pounds, Mason had an intimidating physical presence that made meeting his eyes no small feat. But Soren's natural defiance overrode whatever common sense should have told him not to antagonize Mason. "I don't have to stay," he said.

"You're not going anywhere. You're staying put. You earn your keep. You do as I say and when I say it. You don't try to swim back. You won't come up with any harebrained schemes to make me bring you back. And I should warn you. I was trained as a field medic." Mason slapped his hand on the breakfast bar. "Short of brain surgery, I'll do it all right here."

Soren studied the large man for a long moment, his gaze sliding over the tanned face. Under full brows, Mason's eyes were so dark, there was no telling where his pupils ended and his irises began. "You've got to be kidding me."

He remembered the way Mason had gently slathered his bruises with soothing cream. He thought he could still feel Mason's fingers cupping his chin. He had no doubt Mason would tie him to the breakfast counter and take his appendix out if the need arose. Damn him. Smug bastard.

The water inside the kettle on the stove began to boil.

"Got any sugar to go with that tea?" Soren asked.

The answer was no.

Soren shouldn't have been surprised when Mason declared he had no sugar on board. None whatsoever. But if Soren had known then, seven days ago, what he knew now, he'd have begged Ben for a ride out of there. Hell, he'd have thrown himself into the Pacific while the coastline of Guam was still visible.

But he'd stayed with Mason who drank his tea Japanese-style—bitter and refreshing—abstained from refined sugars and didn't believe in television. The man lived a truly freakish lifestyle.

Mason was a morning person, going to bed early and rising before dawn. The fact that Soren was a night owl who didn't usually climb into his upper bunk until way past midnight and subsequently didn't enjoy getting out of bed before noon didn't keep Mason from waking him up at the crack of dawn.

Mason's while-I-watch-the-sun-rise routine included chin-ups, a leisurely eighty push-ups and eighty sit-ups in two minutes, respectively, and a fifteen-minute shower. Soren, who was ready in a fraction of that time, broke out in a sweat just thinking about exercise before breakfast.

Even their grooming habits were completely different: Mason's dark hair was precisely cut, a habit left over from his Army Ranger days. Soren's copper hair had outgrown its last haircut months ago, and half the time he didn't bother yanking a comb through the tousled red mop.

Mason enjoyed his morning (and sometimes evening) ritual of lathering up and scraping beard stubble from his face, which he followed up with facial moisturizers. Soren couldn't be bothered with shaving every day. Bringing a sharp blade near his throat probably wasn't a good idea any time of the day. And the only cream that touched his skin had an SPF of 50.

In fact, while Soren was into layers—his fair skin didn't reward sunbathing—Mason wore nothing but canvas shorts.

They weren't all opposites, though.

They both missed alcohol: Mason a good glass of wine after dinner or while sitting on the foredeck, watching the sun sink below the horizon, and Soren any time of the day to dull his boredom.

They swam and snorkeled and, much to Soren's surprise, Mason had no problems lazing away an hour or two in the shade of the covered aft deck, where Soren spent most of his time, lounging in a comfortable deck chair, reading one of Mason's many books out of sheer desperation.

But they bonded over the beautiful teak paneling throughout the boat, the hidden storage nooks and crannies, and the cleverly arranged shelves that kept Mason's books and CDs from spilling to the floor should the boat pitch and roll in rough waters. Soren marveled at the craftsmanship and work that had gone into the cabinetry, immensely pleased that his keen eye and interest surprised and impressed Mason.

The Sea Sprite, he had no trouble admitting, was a very fine boat. A classic, in fact. She'd been condemned to the dry dock when Mason found her. It had taken Mason, Ben and the cabinetmaker two years to gut, restore and reconfigure her to suit Mason's needs.

Just as they were getting along, though, Mason had to ruin it by reminding Soren that when he'd designed his home-style galley he'd forgone a dishwasher in favor of an additional freezer, a fact he brought up without fail right before he assigned dishwashing duty to his guest.

In Soren's estimation, Mason enjoyed bossing him around entirely too much. Wash the dishes! Rinse the snorkel gear! Drive the Sprite! Learn to use the radio in case of an emergency! Memorize Ben's phone number! Pick up after yourself!

But while Mason might have expected military-like obedience, Soren did nothing without first questioning it. Soon their routine included a variation on the same conversation:

"I don't see why I have to do that."

"Because I told you so."

"I'm a guest. I should be treated with respect."

"Right," Mason would drawl, his voice dripping with sarcasm. "On my boat, I'm the captain. I give the orders."

Soren had yet to come up with a good counter argument.

And that was precisely why he was in the galley, staring down at the mahi mahi he'd caught that afternoon. The fish's sightless eyes peered up at him from the cutting board, and Soren wasn't hungry anymore. He was okay with catching his own dinner—fishing beat doing the dishes hands down—but gutting his catch? He grumbled and shot Mason a dark look over the counter that separated the galley from the salon.

Mason, the smug bastard, grinned from ear to ear. He was stretched out on his custom-fitted couch that hugged the starboard side of the Sprite's salon, looking comfortable and not the least bit interested in helping Soren.

"You do it," Soren said, putting down the flat knife. "I'll do the damned dishes."

Mason shook his head, closed his eyes and turned his face toward the sunlight streaming in through open blinds. "You've seen me do it a dozen times. I have total confidence in you."

Soren snorted. "Come on. I catch. You cook. I do the dishes. Seems fair."

Mason cracked open an eye, his gaze meeting Soren's plea with a renewed shake of his head and an even wider grin. "Will you quit negotiation and just gut the damn fish?"

Soren bit back a curse and slid the knife into the fish like he'd been shown. He grimaced the entire time he cleaned and filleted their dinner, vowing never to get suckered into fishing again.

"Now be honest," Mason challenged after they'd eaten what had turned into a fine grilled meal, "isn't this better than having someone set a plate in front of you?"

Soren shrugged. He felt Mason's gaze on him and decided to go on the offensive. He rose from his stool at the counter and stretched, fully aware of the espresso-colored eyes that followed his movements.

But Mason wasn't that easily distracted. "You don't feel the slightest sense of accomplishment?"

"You must think I'm an inept, spoiled brat."

Mason shrugged. "No need to sugarcoat it for me."

"You don't get it."

Mason walked around the long counter into the galley and helped himself to a bottle of water from his fridge. "So explain it to me," he pushed.

Soren dropped down on the massive couch. He rested his head on the armrest and looked up at Mason, still in the galley. He watched Mason's throat work as he drank and licked his own dry lips. "Independence and self-sufficiency might have been valued in your family. It's more of a four letter word where I come from."

Mason shook his head. "You're right, I don't get it."

Soren opened his mouth to defend a life he didn't particularly enjoy, but Mason held up a hand and stopped him in his tracks. He found his stool again and leaned back against the counter. "I get the idea that your father kept you dependent. Fine. But what I don't get is why you're hiding behind him."

Soren's eyes narrowed.

"You're making excuses," Mason continued. "I'm not trying to be judgmental here, Soren. I understand where you're coming from, but I thought you were here because you don't want to go back there. Not to your father's house and not to whatever situation you were in."

Soren gritted his teeth. In a drunken fit of spite against his father, he'd climbed out of his bedroom window, went to the FBI and landed on the Sprite. He couldn't say that he'd given his future much thought.

Mason seemed to have done that, though. "Quit using his methods to keep you dependent on him and his money to hide behind. Make a decision for yourself. This is your life now. If you're going to buy frozen fish sticks from now on, that's fine with me, but stop blaming your father for the choices you are making now."

Soren made a face and pushed a hand through his tangled hair. Really, he tried to avoid thinking of his future as much as possible, but Mason, like a terrier with a ball, kept bringing it up. His only recourse: the lapse into brooding silence.

"Ben is stopping by tomorrow," Mason said eventually. "Bringing supplies."

"Oh?"

"Yes, and I believe he said he had something to help you cope."

Soren dragged the Gameboy Mason's nephews had left behind out from under the couch. "Batteries?"

"He didn't say." Mason got to his feet. "Just how long did it last?"

"I almost made it to the championship game," Soren wouldn't have chosen the soccer game for himself, but while it lasted it had served its purpose, keeping him entertained and thought-free for an hour or two.

"I'm turning in, kid."

Soren nodded and waved Mason away, but his eyes remained on Mason's broad back until his host disappeared down the steps and hallway that led to his stateroom. Soren had to give the guy credit—Mason was in great shape for a man his age, which Soren guessed to be in his early thirties. He wondered if Mason slept in the nude.

Soren felt his hormones take notice at the thought and groaned. He could not be held responsible for his growing interest. It was boredom, pure and simple. Watching Mason work out and glide into the Pacific for a swim was his only entertainment. Of course, he'd begin to wonder what all those muscles rolling and flexing under tanned skin would feel like against his body. Then his mind would wander and the next thing he knew, he'd be imagining what it would feel like to be under the solid weight of that glorious body.

Hard, he figured, reaching into his shorts to adjust himself. Rock-hard.

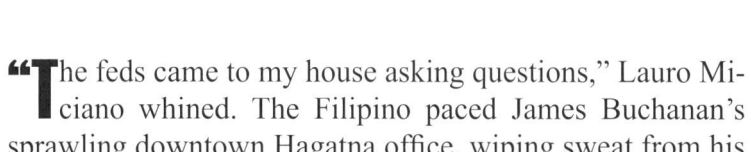

"The feds came to my house asking questions," Lauro Miciano whined. The Filipino paced James Buchanan's sprawling downtown Hagatna office, wiping sweat from his brow with a handkerchief.

Officially, Miciano, who'd been naturalized decades ago, supplied furniture, antiques and souvenirs from the Philippines to local gift shops. Unofficially, he traded money and information with the kind of people who were classified as terrorists these days.

"It is a scare tactic." James did not bother looking up from his laptop. On his list of immediate concerns, Miciano's panic ranked near the bottom. "You are clean," he assured his client. "The hearings are a formality. In your case, they are not worth losing sleep over."

"Feds, James, feds. At my house."

A quick tightening of the lips betrayed James's annoyance. He closed his files and shut down the laptop, before he pushed away from his desk. He got up to fix his client and himself a drink, dropped ice cubes into French crystal tumblers and filled the glasses with Perrier bottled water. "Trust me. They can have their forensic accountants look all they want."

James Buchanan, an accountant himself, knew what he was talking about. As a boy from upstate New York, he had come to Guam with the Navy and promptly fallen madly in love with a beautiful, tawny-skinned native Chamorro girl with dark, soulful eyes. They had married, and after his time in the military, he had made Guam his home and gone into business for himself.

Forty years later, James was the proprietor of a large and exclusive accounting firm. He had been mayor of Mangilao for two consecutive terms, was on the Hagatna City Council and on a first-name basis with the governor. He had regular dinners with the business elite and played golf with the president of one of the richest banks in Guam. James was in his early sixties, but thanks to a strict workout regimen and diet, he looked no older than fifty. He had a mop of stark white hair, blue eyes that had lost some of their brilliance with age, and a trademark smile, which he had whitened on regular business trips back to the U.S. mainland. There was no one on the island who knew more clever ways to evade taxes or invest the proceeds of illegal activity.

Then the governor's chief of staff had been indicted with bank fraud, conspiracy to commit bank fraud, three counts of money laundering and one count of conspiracy to commit money laundering. Amateur!

Now the Department of Justice and its financial investigations taskforce was scrutinizing the bank the governor's man had worked with, as well as her clients and customers. It just so happened that James did a lot of business with the same bank, legally and illegally.

Lauro gulped down the water and resumed his pacing. "I know. I know. I trust you." He loosened his tie and raked a hand through his thinning hair.

"What is it then?"

"It's Jolina."

James's widening smile was a reflex. He could not stand the crazy bitch, was in fact only catering to her whims because her connections made him a lot of money. "And how is your lovely niece?"

Lauro grimaced.

James took pleasure from the man's discomfort. While lovely was certainly a way to describe Jolina, dangerous and volatile were better fitting adjectives. Unfortunately, she regularly came to Guam to visit and party. In fact, she had only just left, rather abruptly, after yet another fight with Soren who was her favorite pastime while on Guam. He had no qualms about introducing her to his rich friends, but he staunchly refused to sell her drugs to them, which made it a constant source of friction.

James was certain his son would reconcile with the temperamental Filipina. Their latest break-up was nothing more than a spat, a short-lived quarrel. James thought he had made that abundantly clear. He still remembered their conversation the night before he had had to beat some sense into Soren.

"You better be at the hotel tonight," James had snapped at Soren, his patience spent. "You will drool all over Jolina. And after dinner, while I discuss business with Lauro, you better fuck her senseless. That is if you are man enough to hold your liquor and get it up."

Alcohol was not the problem, James knew. His son seldom returned home sober after a night of partying. Whatever the reasons for Soren's increasing disinterest in Jolina—what reasons could a healthy young man have to balk at bedding a beautiful woman?—he would have to get over them. "By God, son, if you fuck this up for me, if she complains again that you are not receptive to her charms, you will regret coming home."

He already thought he would have to beat some understanding into Soren the next morning. That boy would entertain Jolina whether he wanted to or not; nothing else was acceptable. "Be there. Tonight. At the hotel. Jolina is expecting to get laid. And I am expecting you to oblige her."

Of course, Soren had not done as he was told. Indeed, the news that he had had the nerve to dump Jolina proved to James what he had suspected all along: his son sorely lacked the proper perspective.

James had not thought much of Soren's absence since that morning. He often disappeared for a time after one of their arguments, but had it been a week already?

"What about Jolina?" he asked Lauro, stopping the man's sweaty pacing in front of his desk.

"She's back."

"I will be sure to tell Soren."

Now he understood Lauro's concern. The legal money Lauro sent to the country of his birth ended in the illegal hands of his niece, who then funneled it to her cousins, who in turn used the funds to arm themselves. They may have started out as communist rebels, fighting a government busy hunting down Islamist separatists, but in truth they were barely more than common criminals interested only in robbery, extortion and kidnapping for ransom.

The thought of Jolina, her drugs, and possibly her cousins who enjoyed partying as much as she did, under Lauro's roof with the chance of a return visit from federal agents at the same time made James's stomach churn.

Lauro set his glass down on the desk where it was sure to leave an unsightly watermark and collapsed into the leather chair before the desk. "I don't like this. I don't like this at all."

James snatched the tumbler off his desk and carried it to his bar. It was after hours, and it was late. The offices of his employees were dark, the hallways abandoned. He wanted to go home, not listen to Lauro Miciano whine.

"Tell me again what happened."

Lauro recounted for the second time a short and routine

visit from a federal agent with a few simple questions, none of which worried James.

"Like I said, just a formality. Why do you not go home and let me worry about your money, Lauro? Our dealings with the bank will stand up to any scrutiny."

Lauro sighed and heaved himself out of the leather chair. He dabbed at the sweat on his upper lip with his kerchief and forced a smile. "You will tell Soren about Jolina?"

"I sure will," James promised and saw Miciano out.

At the door, James nodded at the man responsible for his personal safety. He was not more than an intelligent, barrel-chested thug, but a spiffy title immediately improved his credibility.

After all, James Buchanan did not surround himself with thugs and hooligans. His impeccable daytime reputation and community standing would suffer. Thus, he employed a chief security officer, a bodyguard and several security specialists. Never mind that none of his goons knew the first thing about professional personal security.

No, his men were more useful collecting on the loans James graciously provided to a less than law-abiding cross section of the Guamanian population that could not or would not find legitimate banking for their business ventures.

"I do not care where he is or how you do it. Find Soren," James ordered. He did not ordinarily care about Soren's whereabouts, especially not after one of their altercations. Soren would go off, sulk, lick his wounds, and, after a few days, reappear. He would remember who paid his bills and financed his lazy lifestyle and come home.

Maybe James should have paid more attention to his men's report that Soren had been seen entering the Maite Branch First Hawaiian Bank Building, which housed the FBI's local offices.

James was not sure, could not be sure, if an information exchange had been initiated between his wayward son and the FBI. Who had approached whom first? Had the feds gotten to his son? Had Soren betrayed him out of spite? One thing he was certain of, Soren did not bank with First Hawaiian.

It was not as if James was asking for much. Truly, he was not in the habit of interfering with his children's lives as long as they kept their priorities straight. Active interest in the family business was the least he could expect. Soren, of course, had other ideas. Who knew what his priorities were?

It was clear to James what his son's priority should be: Jolina. Keeping Lauro's crazy niece happy while she visited was the least Soren could do for the family business. It was not as if she was an unattractive, unappealing young woman. Keeping her happy and in a forgiving mood was important, because it kept Lauro, a man easily rattled, from worrying and attracting undue attention.

Now Jolina, who had flown back to the Philippines, had returned quicker than anticipated and she'd probably brought her no-good cousins with her.

Unlike most of the people James did business with—dubious Japanese and Filipino businessmen among them—the outfit Jolina ran with was skittish enough to do away with complications. The bank hearings were a minor complication. Miciano sweating every time he saw a federal badge was a minor complication. Soren talking to the feds was a major complication, though. Not only did he know about his father's daytime and nighttime books, he also knew whatever Jolina had shared with him about her daytime and nighttime activities.

If Soren had indeed become a snitch, then he was in for some unpleasant surprises.

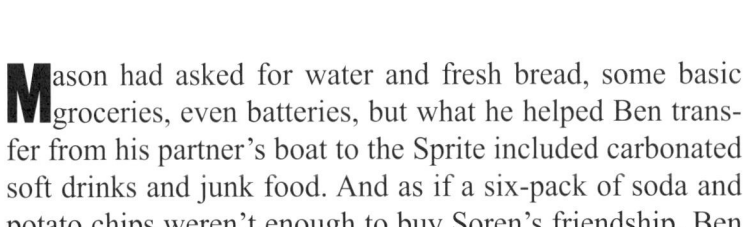

Mason had asked for water and fresh bread, some basic groceries, even batteries, but what he helped Ben transfer from his partner's boat to the Sprite included carbonated soft drinks and junk food. And as if a six-pack of soda and potato chips weren't enough to buy Soren's friendship, Ben had also brought a jar of instant coffee.

"This," he announced with some reverence, "is Douwe Egberts Continental Dark. Freeze dried to perfection." He grinned and handed the glass jar with the dark label over the counter to Soren. "I have a friend who supplies me with these straight from the UK. Probably the world's best instant coffee." He winked. "A cup of this makes getting up in the morning worthwhile."

Soren sighed, clutching the glass jar like newly discovered treasure.

Mason rolled his eyes.

"Ignore him," Ben said. "He wouldn't know a good cup of coffee if it bit him on the ass."

"Can't I come live with you?"

"Heavens no." Ben gestured wildly and shook his head. "I got a new wife. I can't bring a good-looking kid like you home with me."

Mason snorted, stowing cheese and milk away in his fridge. "What he's trying to say is that he's afraid his wife might change her mind once she sees you." He knew the chances of that happening were nil. Ben's wife had been married to the man for almost twenty years and no redhead half her husband's age would change her mind. Not even a redhead of Soren's caliber.

"Wives do that. Change their minds," Soren said. "Or so my father says."

"What else does he say?" Ben wondered.

Mason didn't need to see the small laugh lines around Ben's eyes straightening out to recognize something was up. He could hear it in his friend's voice. He closed the fridge where he'd made room for Soren's six-pack of liquid tooth-rot—he doubted the redhead would thank him—and tuned in to the conversation.

Soren raised his brows and fixed Ben with an innocent look. "What do you mean?"

Oh, he was good! Mason suppressed a grin. Unlike Ben, who hadn't spent the last seven days cooped up with the kid, he knew that expression of false innocence.

Ben, though, apparently wasn't buying Soren's act either. He scratched his stubbly chin, a gesture Mason was as familiar with as Soren's puppy-dog look. "Kaoru wouldn't say," he admitted, "but it's obvious what he wanted Mason to believe."

Mason's brows shot up. "Oh?"

"Unless you were off island the last couple of weeks,

you've heard about that bank fuck-up. And there's just no way you could have missed all the discussions surrounding dear old dad's connection to the bank and the governor and his idiot chief of staff."

Soren nodded.

Mason nodded.

Ben went on. "So we've all heard the news. Then Kaoru says he's got you. He won't say, but he's investigating something." He rolled his eyes. "I mean come on. It is so obvious what he wants us to believe. You rolled over on your father. No question about it. After the way he treated you, it makes sense."

What made less sense, Mason thought, was Kaoru's decision to stash the redhead away with him. Soren, the witness to his father's money laundering and dealings with the Hagatna Commercial Bank, should have been quite safe in the hands of the FBI. Kaoru could have tasked one of his federal co-workers with Soren's protection. Instead he'd called Mason, who was not in the business of protecting people.

After his separation from the Army, Mason had taken his specialized skills to Malaysia, becoming a casino/hotel security manager. He'd loved his job and he'd been good at it, but he wanted to return home. Guam wasn't exactly teeming with job opportunities, though. Then Ben had gotten in touch with him. Mason's boyhood friend from down the block had inherited his father's small security company, a business on the verge of bankruptcy. Armed with a plan, but not much else, Ben had called the one man he knew who had the skills and talents Ben needed. It hadn't taken much to talk Mason into a partnership.

Months later, they founded Security Solutions. Whereas Ben's father had provided monitoring systems, Mason and Ben offered uniformed guard services. Their employees now protected small businesses, industrial buildings, and a few of the many hotels. They roamed the Tumon Bay Mall, patrolled the grounds of the University, and generally did the best they could to keep a lot of Guam's commercial properties safe.

Yes, Mason occasionally did favors for his old friends or their cousin's friends that could be construed as bodyguarding, and he taught personal safety classes, but on the whole he wasn't in the business of protecting people. Kaoru knew that.

The way Mason saw it, there were only two certain facts: Kaoru trusted him, and the situation his friend was dealing with was an unusual one.

Soren studied the dark label on the coffee jar, and Mason wondered if he'd indeed rolled over on his father. Why else would he need protection?

"Here is what I think," Ben began when it became obvious Soren wasn't going to break down and spill his secrets. "You're the ace up Kaoru's sleeve. Unfortunately, you're also a drunk and a recreational junkie." He tore into the bag of potato chips, absently offering it to Mason—who curled his lip at the fatty snack—before fishing out a chip for himself.

Soren shrugged.

Mason tried not to smile. A week ago the redhead would have gone on the defensive, which was probably what Ben had also expected, judging by his hesitation.

"Yeah, well, an angry son with a drug problem doesn't make for a very credible witness."

"So?"

"So Kaoru knows that. He tries to fly you under the radar. He'll exhaust all his other options first, bringing you out of hiding only when and if he has to. Maybe you're not so much his ace, as his backup."

Mason met Soren's jade-colored glance and had the sudden notion that Ben's speculations were closer to the truth than his friend realized.

"Kaoru's trying to do you a favor, or so he told Mason," Ben continued. "Officially, he keeps you out of his investigation, and you won't have to rat out your own father. But I think there's something else going on."

"Like what?"

"Did you contact Kaoru or did he find you?"

"I found him."

"Ready to spill family secrets?"

"Yes."

"Because you're a pissed off, angry son."

Soren didn't bother replying. The bruises on his face were still visible.

"You tell him what you know. He recognizes you're not a good witness. But he can't send you home. Out of the goodness of his heart, he stashes you here."

"Right," Soren said.

Frustrated, Ben reached into the bag of chips again, munching the snack he'd bought for Soren. "I'm just not buying it," he said. "I can't put my finger on it, but there's something you're not telling."

Mason had to agree with his friend, but judging by the puppy-dog expression that settled across Soren's features, the redhead wasn't going to volunteer his truth.

What kind of family secret had he given up? Mason was beginning to wonder if The Smile had anything to do with Soren's exile on The Sprite at all. "What exactly did you tell Kaoru?"

Soren raised his eyes from the coffee label and met Mason's stare head on. "I told him about my father's business with Hagatna Commercial."

6

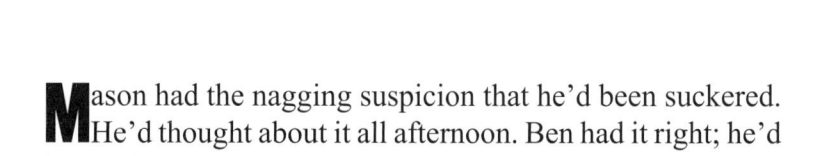

Mason had the nagging suspicion that he'd been suckered. He'd thought about it all afternoon. Ben had it right; he'd jumped to conclusions and something just didn't add up.

He'd taken Soren's story at face value. Battered son, asshole father. Perversely, the fact that Soren met his eyes didn't make him feel any better. He had to remind himself that The Smile's son would have learned how to lie without batting an eyelash from his father.

The fact that Ben had more to say on the subject didn't bode well either. They'd saddled Soren with the task of grilling dinner out on the sundeck and retreated to the privacy of Mason's office. Where Ben wedged the upholstered visitor's chair in the corner so he could prop his feet up on the desk without having to fold in on himself. "Christ, my closet is bigger than this."

"So's mine." Mason smirked. "Now, what's so important we had to do this behind closed doors?"

"He's lying."

"Who? Soren?" Mason widened his eyes with comic surprise and dropped his jaw. "No way!"

Ben shot him a dubious look and huffed. "We're not talking money-laundering here," he said with conviction.

"Buchanan's a crook. We know that. The law knows that." Mason shrugged. He was a newspaper reader. He knew the government had probed The Smile's business dealings before, unsuccessfully. It wasn't enough to prove he had a criminal client, or a dozen of them. Not even if the entire world knew his client's money wasn't earned through hard work and legal sweat. Unless the feds were able to link Buchanan's clients to specific crimes and the income from those crimes to the money Buchanan laundered … details garnered convictions, not generalizations.

Ben nodded. "Okay, but listen to this. Kaoru calls, asks us, well, you, to keep Soren out of sight. We, and by that I mean you, buy 'It's for his own safety' and immediately associate The Smile with those bank hearings next month."

"We just discussed that."

"Right. But I'm thinking this has nothing to do with the Hagatna Commercial Bank. It's a smoke screen. Under the pretense of looking into that whole money laundering business and the Buchanan connection, the feds quietly take Soren aside and use his inside information to go after the real target. This whole bank fuck-up gives them the perfect excuse to take a closer look at Buchanan, when in reality their eyes are on his clients."

Mason sat back in his chair, propped his own feet up and raised a dark brow, encourageming Ben to continue. His friend had a tendency to stop for dramatic pauses.

"I did some digging, and Buchanan is doing business with some shady Filipinos. Terrorists, Mason. My source—"

"Your source?" The tilt to Mason's mouth was clearly skeptical. Ben's sources weren't what Mason would call credible, even though their gossip and speculations had a fairly high degree of accuracy.

"Yes, my source." Ben dug a piece of folded paper out of the leg pocket of his cargo shorts. He smoothed out the wrinkled page and handed it over. "Check out the picture. Soren with his on-again, off-again squeeze. Her name's Jolina Miciano. She's not only rumored to have ties to a group of terrorists back in the Philippines, but she's also related to one of The Smile's clients."

Mason took a look at the page torn from the local gossip rag that was available in vending machines all over the island, when Ben's words caught up with his momentary distraction. "Terrorists?"

"It's simple, really. Buchanan's Filipino client uses perfectly legal money to help out some charity back home. There is nothing wrong with that. Only, the charity isn't really a charity and the money actually funds his extremist friends who want to blow our heads off. Terrorists, Mason. And Soren has the scoop on their local guy."

"How much of this theory of yours is based on actual facts?"

"It makes perfect sense. Since the money is legal and the accounting is legal, Buchanan doesn't have to worry about that bank business hearing unearthing anything to give him a headache. But the feds have an in and their snooping isn't questioned."

Mason thought about that for a few moments. It did make sense. Although, it might have only made sense because he was familiar with the way Ben's brain worked. And while it answered some questions, it posed others. Had Kaoru suggested taking Soren out on the Sprite because he knew the threat was greater than he led on? No, that made no sense. What possible reason would his friend have for downplaying a threat?

"All this because Soren lied and The Smile's in business with a Filipino who has questionable relatives?"

"Hey"—Ben shrugged—"it could be that the FBI is just paying us to keep Soren from getting smacked around. That way he can eventually testify about the couple hundred illegal Ks his father used to buy savings bonds. Little fish need to be nabbed, too."

"Could be," Mason murmured. "Could be." In fact, it was far more likely, Mason figured. Kaoru had been quite clear. He'd wanted Soren, who was somewhat unpredictable, as far away from his father and the source of his unpredictability as possible. He'd wanted Soren out of reach of his violent father, not protected from terrorists.

"I'm telling you, Mason," Ben insisted, "there is something else going on. I have this feeling. If Soren went to Kaoru with dirt on The Smile, he'd be under proper federal supervision, protective custody and what not. But he's not. He's here. Whatever he gave Kaoru, I have a feeling has nothing to do with this official bank investigation. Kaoru couldn't send him back, but he can't put him in custody either. Why?"

Mason shook his head. No, if Soren had come to Kaoru with information about an American businessman financing terrorist activities in the Philippines, if all that stood between Soren and that group of terrorists was a girlfriend, he wouldn't be on the Sprite. If indeed there were terrorists, which Mason doubted very much. Whose story would he trust? Kaoru's, or Ben's gossipy source?

"Think about it," Ben suggested. He stood and began rummaging through his pockets until he found a beaten strip of chewing gum.

Mason's eyes kept straying to the wrinkled magazine page with Soren's photograph. He didn't think the redhead had been aware of the camera, talking to someone outside the shot. But the young woman at his side beamed straight at the photographer. She was model-skinny and beautiful. Not exactly the embodiment of a terrorist, Mason thought. "What's the word on the street? Anyone looking for Soren?"

"I haven't heard anything. I don't think The Smile's looking. By the way, your mom sends her love." Ben chuckled. "I told her you were out cruising redheads. I don't think she got it." He grinned and pushed at his glasses. "Now can we please go see what trouble my steak is in?"

Mason was still thinking about the Smile's lack of concern for his son when they stepped on the sundeck where Soren was standing by the grill, a grilling fork in one hand and binoculars in the other.

"What are you doing?" Ben squinted in the direction Soren was looking and saw a small yacht bobbing on the waves.

"Checking out a chick who's sunbathing topless."

"Let me see." Ben took the binoculars, raised them to his eyes and whistled. "Nice. Very nice." He jammed his elbow in Soren's ribs and nodded his chin at the steaks on the grill. "Mind those, kid."

Soren grumbled good-naturedly.

Mason silently reached over and appropriated the binoculars. He wasn't interested in the brunette lying on deck—who wasn't topless at all—but his glance swept over the lines of the boat. "I know her," he said. "The boat," he added with a quick, chilly sideways look at his partner and Soren. "It's a charter. Usually moors next to the Sprite."

Ben frowned. "Neighbors?"

Mason lowered his binoculars and fixed his friend with a somber look. Ben mirrored his seriousness.

"Coincidence?"

7

Mason had been sound asleep until Soren tumbled into his bed. Suddenly Mason was awake and aware. Soren's hands on him. Soren's bony elbow jabbed him in the gut, low enough that he reflexively shifted to protect his crotch from the falling figure that followed the elbow.

In an effort to push himself off the bed, Soren managed to crawl over Mason. He cursed and his breath fanned warmly across Mason's chest.

Mason's arousal was immediate.

Despite the dark, Mason's hands unerringly found Soren's shoulders and shoved the unwelcome body to his side, away from his swelling crotch. "What the hell?"

"Are you sleeping naked?"

Mason growled deep in his throat, already sliding out from under the thin sheet. Yes, he was sleeping naked, but that didn't stop him from reaching for the lamp at his bedside table.

"Soren, I swear—"

A grating noise very much out of place on the open ocean interrupted Mason's outbreak.

"Listen," Soren whispered.

Mason did, hand hovering over the light switch. He heard the rush of blood through his veins, the pounding of his heart and his ragged breathing. Then, slowly, other sounds started to drift through the open ports: the gentle lapping of waves against the hull of the Sprite and the very distinctive grating of PVC and foam fenders as they rubbed against a second hull.

"Remember your neighbor from the marina? The charter yacht? They pulled up along side," Soren whispered, confirming what Mason already knew. They had company.

"You sure it's them?"

"Yes."

Mason cursed. After dinner, he'd motored the Sprite south. Ben, who'd followed him at a distance, had kept an eye on the charter yacht and her sunbathing guest for as long as his binoculars allowed. They'd spent the evening scanning the horizon, but there had been no sign of the charter yacht again. Until now.

"What time is it?"

"Two."

"Christ. When do you go to bed?"

In the dark, the sound of a drawer being pulled open was as unmistakable as the sound of a mag clip sliding into a handgun, which was followed by the rustle of fabric as Mason pulled on the shorts he'd shed hours earlier.

"Stay. Don't leave. I mean it, Soren."

For a man well over six feet and two hundred pounds, Mason could move with the stealth of an alley cat. He lacked the feline's night vision, but after having gutted and rebuilt the interior of the Sprite and having lived on her for years,

Mason was at home on his boat even in the dark.

Silently, he slid into the passageway and peered into the darkness. The Beretta in his hand—a weapon he'd known as the M9 in his Army days—was a familiar if not often used weight. He didn't plan on using it now, but he wouldn't hesitate to pull the trigger.

After a long moment Mason crept up the five stairs and slipped fluidly into the shadowy galley. It wasn't as dark on this level of the Sprite—the galley sidedeck door stood open and the blinds hadn't been closed—but he knew how to blend into the shadows. And the man in his living room, silhouetted against the back door he'd opened to come in, had his back turned.

His uninvited guest cautiously moved around.

Mason saw nothing in the intruder's hands and slid his gun into the waistband of his shorts—he didn't want to shoot an unarmed person. The metal was cool against the bare skin of his lower belly. For a fleeting moment he allowed himself the luxury of remembering the almost violent reaction of his body to Soren's breath on his chest. He reflexively adjusted himself in his shorts.

Damn, if anyone was going to kill the kid, it was him. And Soren would deserve it. For teasing him in the cut-offs and surfer shorts he'd had to borrow from Mason's closet. They were too large on Soren's lean frame and, without a belt, kept slipping lower and lower. Soren didn't seem to mind, while Mason expected the shorts to drop to the kid's ankles with the next exhale. It had yet to happen, but Mason was convinced it would. Sooner or later. It didn't help at all that he knew Soren wore nothing underneath those shorts. Damn tease.

Mason peered back down the dark passageway, not entirely convinced Soren would do as he'd been told. The hallway, though, appeared undisturbed and empty.

Concentrating on his approaching intruder, Mason listened to soft footfalls on the parquet floor. On cat's feet, he left the galley through the open side door, stole along the side deck, shot a quick look at the charter yacht—she appeared abandoned, but he didn't feel comfortable leaving the Sprite to investigate—and slid into his living room from the aft deck. He heard a muffled thud and faint cursing. The Sprite had her share of protruding corners and shin-hazards. If you were tall, you had to know to duck your head to leave the galley. Not surprisingly, the hooded figure that stood by the dark stairs rubbed his bruised forehead.

Mason's grin, which had nothing to do with amusement, widened, then froze as the business end of a gun was pressed against the back of his skull. He didn't wait for the command to straighten or the bullet to end his life. Instead, he reached behind himself, grabbed the legs there, whirled and pulled the gun-happy intruder off his feet all in one quicksilver motion. The man went down and whacked his head on the parquet floor, the force of the impact forcing the air from his lungs. The gun fell from his stunned hand and slid across the floor into the shadowy living room.

Mason lost sight of the gun in the shadows. He was more concerned about the uninvited guest in the galley. He pulled his semi-automatic on the nervous intruder, saw Soren's shadow slide up the stairs from the galley to the pilothouse, and staggered. A kick to the kidneys sent bolts of pain across his midsection and along his spine. A roundhouse kick to the wrist sent his gun flying. A third kick to the knee felled him. He rolled with the fall and was on his feet again, facing his attacker, well and truly pissed.

He had just enough time to register that his gun-happy, kicking intruder was a woman meaning business, judging from the way she held her knife, before the blade came down in a slashing arc, razoring hair off Mason's chest.

With his back to the breakfast counter, Mason had nowhere to go, and she knew it. Dancing in and out of his reach, her knife wove invisible patterns in the air. She scored a hit across Mason's ribcage, slicing through the skin over his heart, making it skip a beat.

But she came too close, and he had his hand around her wrist, his forearm blocking her movement. His other hand shot out and grabbed her by the throat. "I don't think so," he growled. He squeezed viciously, bruising bone and windpipe.

She snarled at him and kneed him in the stomach. She used her free hand to punch him in the chest, where blood made his skin slick, and yanked free. Mason had a good idea what the words she hurled at him meant, when his world exploded. Pain lanced through his skull. Stars danced across his field of vision. His right ear rang. His knee buckled.

He lurched against the counter and blinked away the stars. His vision began graying out, but he was pretty sure he'd caught a glimpse of Soren on the sundeck just outside the door. He shook his head, hoping that Soren would understand. He was having great difficulty remaining upright. His brain rattled inside his skull and the Sprite pitched and rolled under his feet.

Through unfocused eyes, he saw his assailant snatch up his fallen Beretta. She grinned at him, her full attention on his misery. Mason groaned and moaned for her, because if she turned, she'd see Soren's arm sneaking over the backdoor threshold with her forgotten gun. He wasn't sure what her exact orders were—dead or alive?—but he had a pretty good idea that she wouldn't take well to Soren arming himself. He could only hope Soren didn't plan anything stupid with her gun. Like, say, shooting anyone.

Mason's heartfelt groan came just as he crumbled to the floor. The last thing he saw was a gun—his gun—trained on him. He braced himself, heard the shot ring out, but darkness swallowed him up before there could be any searing pain.

8

Soren saw Mason crumple, heard the shot, and screamed, "No!"

The gun in his hand recoiled. The acrid smell of cordite filled his nostrils and the noise of the controlled explosion buffeted his eardrums. But as the bullet he'd fired slammed into the woman's shoulder, spinning her around, his entire focus was on the weapon in her hand.

She snarled something he didn't understand, raised her hand, and he fired again. His second bullet tore through her neck and would have missed her entirely if she hadn't staggered into it.

"Shit." The tall guy who'd clubbed Mason over the head

dove behind the galley counter.

Soren's purely instinctual reaction put a bullet into the refrigerator. This time the recoil was enough to jar him out of his daze. He backpedaled and, not realizing he'd stepped into the salon, tripped over the raised threshold. He sat down hard, the impact rattling his spine up to the base of his skull.

He gulped down a shaky breath of fresh air and caught movement out of the corner of his eye a moment before the second intruder stepped from the narrow ledge that ran along side the Sprite onto the sundeck—the very route Mason and Soren had taken earlier.

Their eyes met over the gun Soren raised, recognition and surprise on both their faces.

"Snitch," the guy mumbled. He spat on the deck and took a threatening step forward.

"I wouldn't," Soren warned, scrambling to his feet, gripping the gun with both hands. Panic started to bloom in the pit of his stomach. He didn't dare glance over his shoulder to check on the woman he'd shot. He could only hope she was out long enough to let him bluff his way out of this. "I'll shoot you, too. We both know your boss won't report you missing."

The tall guy sneered, but stopped advancing.

"How did you find me?"

"Fuck you."

Soren gestured with his gun at the charter yacht gently bumping into the Sprite with each wave. Despite the relative coolness of the night, sweat made his T-shirt clammy and his palms slick. "Tell me how you found me and go."

The tall guy's eyes shone in the dim pre-dawn light as Soren swallowed a curse. Soren knew this guy; the man was a dog trained and conditioned to recognize dominance. "How did you find me?" he yelled, taking a determined step forward, hoping that unlike a dog the intruder couldn't smell his fear.

"We checked out the fed you talked to. Turns out he has a friend with a boat that hasn't been seen for a week. Turns out the friend has a partner. All we had to do was sit on our asses and wait for him to make his move. Then we trailed him."

Soren retreated until he felt the doorjamb against his back and pointed at the charter yacht. "Go."

"What about—"

"I don't think so. Go. Go!"

Soren stayed there, propped up against the doorjamb, gun in a white-knuckled, two-handed grip while the guy left the Sprite. Soren didn't move until the charter yacht disappeared from view. His hands shook, his legs weren't quite as steady as they had been, but he was fine until he turned.

Soren wasn't sure which bloodied body turned his stomach—not that it mattered. He lurched to the railing, hung his head over the side and heaved. When there was nothing but bile dripping into the Pacific, he shrugged out of his shirt and wiped it across his face and mouth. Disgusted, he let it drop into the water, fairly sure Mason wouldn't want it back.

Concern for Mason had him stepping over the threshold. Soren didn't realize he'd left the gun lying on the deck until he saw Mason's Beretta still clutched in the woman's hand. She lay in a puddle of blood where she'd collapsed in front of the couch. Inching toward Mason, Soren kept an eye on her still form, but he couldn't detect any signs of life. He sure as hell wasn't going to go near her to check. Just in case, though, he hurried back out on the sundeck, snatched up her gun, and went to Mason's side.

Mason was still alive. His chest rose and fell with a steady rhythm. He'd crumpled into an uncomfortable sitting position against the counter. Blood seeped through his hair, dripping down the right side of his face, off his chin and onto his bare chest, where a nasty gash bled as well.

Soren swallowed and hurried to grab a towel. He pressed it over Mason's ribs, but immediately snatched his hand away when Mason moaned.

"Shit."

Moving Mason's muscular body was out of the question. Soren would have much preferred to leave the bloody salon, but he wasn't going to drag Mason's dead weight down the stairs, through the hallway and into Mason's stateroom. Instead, with a grunt, he pulled the unconscious man away from the counter and into the galley. Mumbling reassurances, as much to fortify his confidence as to talk to Mason, Soren sat down on the floor and pulled Mason's head into his lap.

"Any time now," he urged, but the large man didn't stir.

Forced to realize he was the only person not incapacitated and had no clue how to work the boat to get them out of there, Soren allowed himself a tight, humorless smile. Oh, sure, Mason had shown him how to drive the Sprite—standing close enough to share his body heat, which hadn't helped Soren's concentration at all—but there was a huge difference between steering the Sprite with her skipper looking over his shoulder, directing him, and finding his own way around the Pacific.

He had a general idea about their location. They'd rounded Guam, traveling north. Occasionally, in the distance, he'd seen glimpses of Rota, one of the Mariana islands. They were somewhere between Guam and Saipan, to the west of the Mariana Trench, which gave Soren the creeps. He enjoyed yachting, but he didn't need to know that 38,000 feet separated him from the ocean floor.

Soren needed help. He extricated himself with great reluctance, but the satellite phone Mason kept for emergencies was in the pilothouse.

It was three in the morning, but Ben must have been sleeping with his ear on the phone, Soren suspected. It only rang once before Ben came on the line.

"What? This better be good."

"Ben? This is Soren—"

"What happened? What time is it? Hold on."

Soren switched the satellite phone to his other ear and took a seat at the Sprite's helm. He didn't want to have this conversation over Mason's unconscious body. When Ben came back on the line, Soren explained what had happened, what he'd seen and that Mason's head was hard enough to dent a toaster oven.

"That doesn't surprise me." Ben chuckled. "Tell me again. You're sure there were only two of them?"

"Yeah."

"Shit. I don't like this. Dammit. You're sure you can't navigate? If I gave you coordinates—"

Grasping the intricacies of latitude and longitude had proved too much for Soren's lazy brain. "I'd end up in the Philippines." So not where he wanted to be.

"I can't believe Mason didn't teach you."

Soren pushed a hand through his hair and grimaced. He'd cheated his way through high school biology, he'd told dates he'd call and hadn't, and once he'd stolen money from his father's wallet (sometimes he still woke up in a cold sweat, fearing his father's wrath). God had sent him Mason to punish him, and true to form, Soren hadn't paid attention. "He tried, okay? It's not like I knew I'd have to do this. Sue me."

Ben relented. "Okay. Okay. Here is what I want you to do. Try to wake Mason up every hour. And when he's not biting your head off, and he will, I want you and your binoculars on deck. You spot anything coming near you that does not look like my boat, you wake up Mason and you get on that radio and call it in. You're sure you remember how to work the radio?"

"Yes." Switches and dials were fine by Soren.

Ben went over his instructions twice more before he was convinced that Soren knew what to do. It was obvious that Ben did not like the situation as it was one bit. "I'm calling Mason's brother. We'll be there as fast as we can."

Armed with Ben's instructions, Soren went back down to the galley. Mason was still out, but not lying quite as still as Soren had left him. His head lolled to the side. He moaned. His eyes moved under their lids. The blood in his hair was beginning to cake over. There were still red smears of it down his face and neck. The cut across his rib still oozed, but he was in no danger of bleeding to death any time soon.

Soren sat and pulled Mason's dark head onto his lap again. He combed his fingers through Mason's short hair, enjoying the large man's warmth. "I'm sorry," Soren mumbled, not entirely sure what exactly he was apologizing for, the lies or his helplessness.

"Not," Mason croaked, bringing his hand up to touch the side of his head, "as sorry as I am."

9

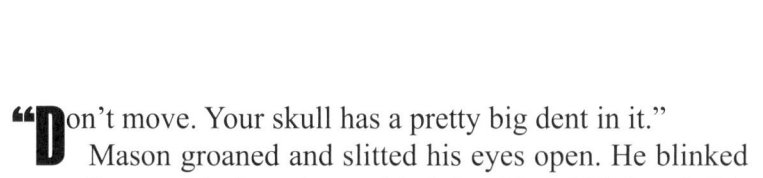

"Don't move. Your skull has a pretty big dent in it."

Mason groaned and slitted his eyes open. He blinked up at Soren and gingerly prodded the side of his head. His fingers came away sticky.

"He tried to brain you with the toaster oven."

"Huh?"

"Toaster oven." Soren jerked his chin in the direction of the fallen appliance.

Mason heaved himself into a sitting position and screwed his eyes shut. Soren saw the muscles in his jaw jump and winced. He had seen the tall guy grab the toaster oven, but he'd also seen Mason shake his head and, in truth, he'd still expected Mason to get himself out of the tight spot he'd been maneuvered into.

He crouched in front of Mason.

"What?"

"How many fingers am I holding up?"

Mason gave him a blank stare. He reached clumsily for the gun lying near Soren's bare feet. "Didn't I tell you to stay put?" He tucked the gun into the waistband of his shorts, wobbled to his feet, and clutched the breakfast counter. "Lucky for you they split." His words were a bit slurred.

Soren's eyes darted in the direction of the couch, then to the gun dragging Mason's shorts dangerously low, past Mason's pronounced tan line. "I don't think you should have that right now." He hooked his fingers inside Mason's waistband and curled his other hand around the butt of the gun resting against Mason's groin—the muzzle had to be poking him in the wrong places. Mason's skin was cold and clammy against his warm fingers.

Mason moaned.

Worried, Soren dropped the gun on the counter and grabbed Mason by the shoulders. "You're okay?"

Mason's expression wasn't that of a man about to pass out, though. A smile more predatory than pleasant twitched his lips. The endless depths of his eyes glinted. Soren recognized the look for what it was, hunger. He dropped his hands and stepped out of Mason's personal space.

"I can't believe a chick kicked your ass," Soren said, mouth suddenly gone dry. "Aren't you supposed to be a professional?"

Mason's eyes snapped up and their gazes locked. Gone was the heat; the espresso-dark brown now frosted over. Soren felt marginally better having that coolness directed at him. There was something unnerving about being mentally undressed when he was already half-naked.

"You need to lie down before you keel over."

"I'm working on it," Mason snapped. His white-knuckled grip on the counter didn't loosen. He craned his neck to peer around Soren. "I'm visualizing."

Soren thought of the intruder's blood staining the carpet in front of the couch and blanched. His stomach clenched, protesting the gentle pitch and roll of the Sprite. He swung his eyes away from the couch and toward the precipitous plunge of the stairs instead. There was no way Mason could manage the steps and long trek to his cabin without falling flat on his face. He wasn't steady on his feet, and his eyes seemed out of focus more often than not. Beneath his darkly tanned complexion, he was ashen. Soren suspected that only sheer willpower kept the man on his feet.

He dreaded the discussion that would inevitably follow Mason's discovery of the dead body sprawled across the living room floor. Just thinking about having to explain his kill started his hands shaking again. He shoved them into the pockets of his borrowed shorts. He needed to keep busy so as not to think about what had happened, what he'd done and, worse of all, what could have happened.

Patching up Mason would do the trick. He knew a thing or two about patching up minor injuries. He knew enough to realize Mason needed more medical care than he could offer: stitches for his side and the hole in his head. Monitored rest. But taping gauze to his wounds would have to hold him over until help arrived. "First aid kit?" Soren asked, voice a bit rough around the edges.

Mason's dark eyes flicked across Soren's shirtless torso again. "Put a shirt on," he growled.

"Excuse me?"

"You heard me. Put a shirt on."

"You're bleeding to death, and you're worried about me not wearing a shirt?"

"Yes."

Just as there were surly drunks, Soren figured, there were surly patients. Mason obviously fell into that category. "Fine."

Glad to be away from the dead woman in the living room, the dented toaster, and the suddenly intense Mason, he stalked off toward his tiny cabin. He took his time choosing between two old, washed-out, extra-large hand-me-downs.

He returned to find Mason swaying over the dead body. Equal parts guilt and wisdom kept Soren in the galley. One didn't offer assistance to surly drunks or surly patients. He waited until Mason collapsed on the couch, then he approached cautiously. "First aid kit?"

Mason's gruff answer was more telling of pain than the little moan he allowed himself. He was determined to hang on to his tough guy image, Soren mused. Mason, the quintessential smug bastard, always in charge and under control. Confident, self-assured and unapologetic Mason. He wondered what it would take to work a moan of a different sort out of the man.

No matter how much Soren wished to think of pleasant pastimes, though, his mind kept replaying what he'd seen while crouched low in the shadows of the aft doors: the fight, her gun skittering across the parquet floor, Mason's large hand clamping around her neck, ready to snap it like a matchstick. She'd been one ticked off broad. Soren knew enough Tagalog to understand a few of the choice words she hurled at her partner before training the gun on Mason. None of them were nice.

Soren gagged. He hung his head over the toilet, retching and heaving. He wasn't prone to panic attacks, and he wasn't particularly squeamish—unless it involved dead fish—but he'd never shot someone before. And the bitch hadn't just fallen over; no, he'd had to shoot her twice.

Still, her death inspired little remorse. What punched the air from his lungs and sent his stomach roiling was the thought of Mason's bullet-riddled body crumpled against the galley counter. A wave of adrenaline threatened to wash Soren's feet out from under him and he clutched at the sink.

"Fuck." He splashed some water on his face and scowled at his reflection in the mirror. He touched his jaw, where the faint evidence of his father's temper still faded away. Yes, he'd asked Kaoru for help getting away from James, but he hadn't thought his father would come after him, or that he would send armed thugs to return him.

Not looking forward to explaining what he knew, Soren found his way back to the salon. Mason had his eyes closed, but he must have gotten up while Soren was gone, because a throw now covered the dead body.

Soren sank on the edge of the couch and watched Mason's impressive chest rise and fall. Even more or less unconscious, Mason was of the tall, dark and handsome sort, despite the dried blood in his hair or his slack mouth. His squared off pecs were separated by a patch of dark hair. His flat stomach, cut into a solid six-pack, was the result of his daily regimen of two hundred sit-ups and crunches (the no-sugar rule probably had something to do with it, too.)

"Did you dump the other one overboard?"

Soren started. "Jesus. I—no." His glower was no match for Mason's. He felt himself blush to the roots of his hair and slid off the couch. He ducked his head, dumped the contents of the battered first aid kit on the floor and rifled through the supplies, determined not to meet Mason's eyes again or be riled by his comments.

"I let him go." He liked to think he'd sent the man home with a message even James would understand: Hands off!

"He'll be back with new friends. More guns."

Soren clenched his jaw in an effort not to defend his actions. It wasn't as if he could have kept his father's goon in line for long. The way he saw it, he'd been incredibly lucky. Keeping the man around would have only made the situation more dangerous. Besides, if Ben hurried, they'd be long gone before James could send more thugs.

"You shot that woman in the back."

"Hey," Soren snapped, his eyes flashing. "You've got, what, a hundred pounds on her, and she still kicked your ass. Damn, that's pretty sad."

Mason glared at Soren.

Soren ignored him. "This might sting." He smacked alcohol-soaked gauze on the lump on the side of Mason's head. "She cut you up before you even had a clue. You should have had her, you know. She was about to shoot you, but I shot her instead. So the way I see it, I saved your sorry ass."

"They didn't come for me," Mason said from between clenched teeth, pulling the gauze away from his split scalp. He leveled a stare at Soren that could have been used to peel paint off the Sprite in dry dock. "They came for you."

10

By the time Ben arrived, Soren was exhausted, Mason's snoring grated on his frayed nerves and the body—he was certain of it—was beginning to smell. Mason had made it very clear: the dead woman wasn't to be touched or moved, something or other about a crime scene. Since he had no wish to get close to her, Soren hadn't paid attention. He did his best to avoid thinking about the fact that he'd taken a life.

Ben must not have shared Mason's concerns. He wasted no time checking over the dead intruder staining the rug. "She's Filipina," he said, looking up at Soren.

"Yeah. So?" Soren fidgeted. This was Guam. Roughly a

third of the population was Filipino. It stood to reason that a few of them weren't law abiding, and that a few of those found employment with his father.

"We need to talk about that." Ben rifled through the pockets of the dead woman and absently nodded over his shoulder at the man blocking the aft doors. "Stoney Ward. Mason's brother."

Soren would have guessed Stoney's family connection without Ben's clarification. He was just as tall as Mason, six four, maybe six five, and just as broad across the shoulders and chest. The muscles under his Hawaiian shirt and washed-out jeans weren't the variety that came from casual gym use. The man had some serious effort invested in his towering body. But unlike Mason, he probably didn't subscribe to GQ magazine. His hair was more tousled than styled. It fell in waves over his ears and touched the collar of his shirt. He hadn't taken the time to shave in days. The hand he clamped on Soren's shoulder wasn't manicured. His fingers were longer, slimmer than Mason's. His face was proportioned differently, but there was enough brotherly resemblance to tell Soren that Mason had a twin.

"You must be the indentured deck hand, huh? Life's tough." Stoney's espresso-brown eyes swept over the corpse at Ben's feet. He winced. "This the chick that kicked Mason's ass?"

"Yeah."

"This crazy old guy," he jerked his stubbly chin in Ben's direction, stepping past the man to reach the couch, "tells me if you hadn't shot her, she would have finished Mason off. That true?"

"Yeah."

"Thanks." He winked. "Let's rub it in when he wakes up." He took one good look at his snoring brother and whistled through his teeth. "Holy shit. That tiny thing there did that? Damn. He's losing his touch."

Soren didn't like the glee in Stoney's voice. Oh, there was concern coloring his voice, too, and his hands were gentle where they checked on the bandages and brushed a dark lock of hair out of the slack face. "Yes, well, there were two of them and the toaster oven."

"Trust me, kid, a horde of them and a washing machine couldn't have gotten a hit in a few years ago." Stoney smiled. "He's still the toughest son of a bitch I know. What about you?"

"What about me?"

"Ever shot anyone before?"

"No."

"Plan on ever shooting anyone again?"

"No."

"Good. Let's keep it that way. I'm a cop, you know. Redhead, huh? Mason married one once. Crazy bitch. Didn't work, of course."

"Why not?" Soren asked. Stoney's energy made him dizzy. He had trouble following the man's conversational leaps. Idly, he wondered if Mason felt that way about him.

Stoney shook his head.

"Well?"

Stoney shrugged. "Mason doesn't swing that way." He straightened. "So, let's talk. Ben made me listen to his harebrained terrorist plot on the way here. The man can talk, I tell you. Anyway. You familiar with his terrorism theory?"

Soren shook his head and let himself be swept into the galley.

"This crazy old guy," Stoney began, stepping over the dented toaster, "thinks your father is in bed with terrorists."

Soren cringed, then nearly started laughing. In bed with terrorists. His father? They had no idea.

"So?" Stoney opened drawers and cupboards until he found the instant coffee. He sniffed at it and grimaced. "So," he nudged again, fixing Soren with an inscrutable look. "Soren, is it? What do you do when you're not Mason's indentured deck hand?"

"Do?"

"Work? You know, what people do to make money and pay bills."

"Oh." Soren hunched his shoulders and grabbed the mug Mason had designated for his coffee use off the counter. He scrutinized the coffee stains inside. He hated being associated with his father's firm, but he hadn't been able to talk his way out of a part-time job there. Then again—his mood lifted at the thought—it was very unlikely that he was returning with all that was going on. "Nothing much. I guess I'm, like, unemployed right now."

"Done any college?"

"Yes." Soren made a face. If the choice had been up to him, he would never have started college. He'd had other plans, but his father had insisted. His sons were to follow in his footsteps. And so Soren had attended the University of Guam. He figured his father wasn't too off the mark: A business degree was a useful thing to have. It had taken him almost two years to work up the nerve to quit. "For a while. I dropped out."

And then he'd run away. His love life had taken a bitter hit and his studies had become tedious and mind-numbing—he really wasn't meant to be an accountant. He'd called his mother in Boston, had bummed money for the airfare off her and had flown halfway across the globe. She'd been ecstatic to spend time with him, even rearranged her busy schedule. She'd talked him into reapplying to the renowned North Bennet Street School. The timing hadn't been right—he'd missed the April deadline by more than six months—but luck had been on his side and in the following February he'd started studying Cabinet and Furniture Making at one of the premier woodworking schools in the country.

His father must not have missed him. Soren liked to think that his father had been quite happy about his absence. When he had finally searched for his son and had heard that Soren studied a trade, he'd been furious. A Buchanan didn't work with his hands, and Soren squandered a perfectly good university education.

He hadn't returned to Guam until after he'd completed his two-year training at North Bennet—much to the chagrin of his father who couldn't go on saying Soren seldom if ever finished what he started. He might not have seen eye to eye with his father, but the large Spanish villa at the outskirts of

Mangilao was still his home, and he much preferred Guam's year-round heat and humidity to Boston's changing and chilly seasons. To appease his father, he'd even taken the part-time position James had had waiting for him.

"So, you're, what, early twenties, college drop-out, still living at home. Your father knocks you around, and you have a thing for booze. No job. Little prospects. I got that right, yeah?" Stoney's expression wavered between boredom and dislike. He shrugged. "Just trying to figure out where you come from," he added.

"And how is this any of your business?"

Stoney laughed. It was a quick, humorless bark, before he slapped his palms on the breakfast counter and leaned forward. "I don't know how things are in your family, but in mine, if you mess with my brother, you mess with me. You put him in harm's way. Intentionally or unintentionally, I don't care. But that makes it my business. Fair enough?"

Soren's chin rose as he met Stoney's espresso-colored glare. "Now what?"

"Now," Ben ambled into the galley, "we drive back." His silvering hair was plastered to his forehead and neck with sweat. His hands were bloody. He went straight to the sink.

Soren watched transfixed as Ben washed his hands. Twice. Then used one of Mason's pristine white towels to wipe the sweat from his brow.

"What about—her?"

"We'll let the police deal with her when we get back. Stoney."

Mason's brother nodded. "I'm here in a semi-official capacity," he explained. "Let me have a sec with Ben and I'll take your statement."

11

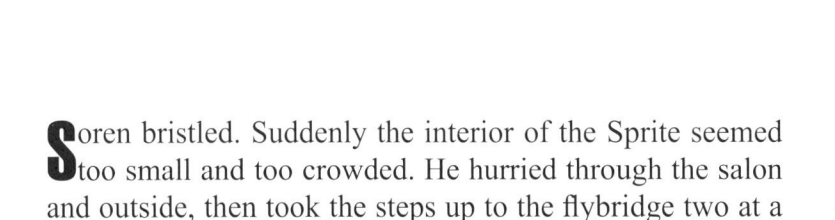

Soren bristled. Suddenly the interior of the Sprite seemed too small and too crowded. He hurried through the salon and outside, then took the steps up to the flybridge two at a time. He dropped on the curved bench, absently noting the moisture that soaked into his shorts, and gulped down fresh air like a man on the verge of drowning.

So Stoney didn't like him. Big deal. He didn't need Stoney's approval, and he wasn't going to be intimidated. But the big man had unwittingly pointed him in the right direction: Ben's suspicion that terrorists were the real threat, while not entirely false, provided all Soren needed to explain away what had happened without admitting to his father's involvement.

Did it make a difference who paid the thugs that had boarded the Sprite? Would his honesty have kept Mason safe? The thought of Mason unconscious and bleeding made Soren's stomach cramp. He surged to his feet and began pacing the small flybridge.

He had no eye for the marvelous rise of the sun over the eastern horizon and no ear for the approach of Mason's brother until Stoney cleared his throat.

"Mason asked me to give this to you," he said, holding out a sweater.

"How is he?"

"He'll be fine. Look, Soren." Stoney crossed his arms and leaned against the bench. "You're right. Whatever you're caught up in, it's none of my business. I don't even care. But my brother was hired to keep you out of sight. Now there's a dead chick on board. You might want to give us a heads up if these people your father works for really are terrorists, because my guess is they might come back and try again."

Soren slipped the green sweater over his head. The scent of Mason enveloping him steadied his nerves and fed his determination. He could still get them all out of this without betraying his father.

"Ben's theory is off the mark," he began. "My father does business with a man named Lauro Miciano, but he's not a terrorist. His niece, Jolina, is. I met Jolina at my father's big Discovery Day bash last March." Just days after he'd returned from Boston. "She's, uh, on the wild side." And sexy as hell. "Drinks a lot. We got drunk and made out." He cringed. Jolina liked sex in public places. She liked the thrill and didn't give a damn about the consequences. Unlike Soren's father, who had been mortified when the hotel manager had shown him an explicit video, courtesy of the penthouse lobby security camera. There had been hell to pay, which resulted in an overnight hospital stay for Soren.

"Jolina … she told me about her cousins back in the Philippines. They extort money from American companies. Mining businesses. Construction. Engineers. For protection, bribes and such. Most pay in order to do business there. They file it under miscellaneous expenses." It was business as usual, apparently. "Some don't pay, but Jolina's cousins, they don't take no for an answer. They kidnap employees for ransom and sometimes send them back missing a few pieces." Soren shuddered, recalling her gleeful explanation about how best to chop off fingers.

Stoney frowned. "She just told you that?"

Soren ducked his head and blushed. "She drinks too much and talks a lot after sex." He shoved his hands into the pockets of his shorts and forced himself to meet Stoney's eyes. "I went to the FBI, told them what I knew and no one cared. They investigated, but nothing ever came of it. Business in the Philippines is good, I guess. But then—" He paused, remembering the fight he'd had with her. "Then she told me she'd killed a man. An accident, she said. I didn't care. I wanted out. I tried to break up with her, she wouldn't listen. I told my father he had to find a different way to keep her and her uncle happy. One thing led to another, and I ended up in Kaoru's office. I told him about the dead guy. I figured you can sweep ransom kidnappings under the rug, but not a dead U.S. citizen. Someone would have to investigate. Kaoru said there wasn't much he could do. I was already flagged as an attention seeker, and his superiors had made it very clear that I was to be turned away next time I showed up."

They heard Ben's rude curse before he reached the flybridge. "So what did Kaoru say?" the man asked.

"I told him I couldn't go back home, and he said he would look into this business with the dead American. If he could find any corroborating information and I managed to stay sober, he might be able to get past his superiors and open an official investigation."

Soren dropped his chin to his chest and stared down at his bare toes. Sex had been grand, but Jolina was a high-strung disaster. Her need for alcohol and the occasional hit of meth had rubbed off on him. His attempts to distance himself hadn't just met with her opposition, no, even his father had expected him to crawl back into her bed.

Ben and Stoney exchanged glances.

"Run me through what happened here. Consider this your official statement."

Soren did. Twice. Leaving out only his recognition of the tall guy with the bruised forehead.

"You've ever seen the dead woman before?"

He shook his head. He had no idea who she was and that was the honest truth.

"Could she have worked for this Jolina chick?"

Soren hesitated. Kaoru had promised him discretion. What were the chances of Jolina knowing that he'd betrayed her confidence? "I wouldn't know."

"What about your father?"

"We're going back, right? Maybe I should just go home. I can patch things up with him. He's—"

"Fuck that," Stoney interrupted, his voice bitter and edgy. "He only hits you when he's had a bad day?" He stood, his shoulders squared, a man fully aware of his height and build. He speared Soren with a dark look he'd cultivated for twelve-year-old drug dealers. "Oh, wait. You provoke him, and you deserve it? You know better, and he's sorry afterwards. At least his wives had the good sense to get out. He ever lay a hand on your mother?"

"That's none of your fucking business."

Stoney relented. "Why didn't she take you with her?" he asked, curious now, the bitter edge to his voice gone.

"I wanted to stay," Soren lied.

"You know what I don't understand, kid?" Ben scratched his sparse beard. "Why do you cower before your father, when you have the courage to break it off with this terrorista? Why do you let him treat you like that?"

Soren took a breath, willed his hands to unclench and his teeth to part with little success. He'd wanted to steer the conversation away from his father's possible involvement, but he wasn't prepared to discuss his victim status. "My father is overbearing and controlling," he said between clenched teeth. "We have arguments, that's all." He yanked a hand ruthlessly through his hair. "Trust me, there won't be a next time. Hell, the last time he beat the shit out of me, I climbed out the damn window and the next thing I know Mason tells me to take my clothes off, because he wanted to play doctor."

Stoney stared at Soren in bafflement. "Play doctor?"

Soren rolled his eye and let out a huff. "He was looking at my bruises."

Stoney chuckled. Ben just shook his head and made a face.

"Oh, you knew what I meant," Soren snapped impatiently.

Stoney composed himself as he held up his hands. "So you're not the spineless victim you seem to be."

"But?"

"But, for the record, going back is a bad idea."

"Amen," Ben agreed. "Now let's get the hell out of here. You're driving the Sprite," he told Stoney and climbed back down the stairs.

Soren watched him get onto his sport fish cruiser. "What happens now? When we get back I mean?"

"I'm calling it in. The coroner will take care of the body. There will be an investigation." Stoney started downstairs, but turned to give Soren a thoughtful look. "I was all for turning you over to Kaoru, but Mason wanted to talk to you first." He smiled to soften the edge of his words. "Ben is taking you guys to his brother-in-law's motel until we figure out who's out to get you."

12

Mason woke up disoriented and thirsty as hell. He was still in his blood-stained shorts, on a bed. The midday sunlight streaming past the half-closed mini blinds irritated his eyes and made his head throb. He vaguely remembered stumbling off the Sprite, getting into Ben's car and driving to the Blue Heaven Motel, a place he'd been to once or twice before. Ben's brother-in-law ran it.

When he lifted his head off the lumpy pillow, exacerbating the throbbing behind his eyes, he could see a second full-sized bed, the sheets rumpled and a shirt that looked suspiciously like Ben's strewn across it. If it was indeed Ben's, then it was probably his partner in the running shower he heard through the closed bathroom door.

It wasn't Soren in the shower, because Soren was lying next to him, asleep, on his side, a knee drawn up, his head pillowed on his outstretched arm.

Mason had to smile despite his splitting headache. He wasn't a social recluse by any means, but it had been a while since he'd woken up next to a warm body.

Even after a week on the Sprite, Soren's porcelain complexion had barely darkened. His freckles, haphazardly sprinkled across his torso, arms, shoulders and every other inch of him, seemed more pronounced. Their chaotic pattern made Mason dizzy.

He reached out and gently brushed the unruly red bangs that always fell into Soren's eyes to the side. Soren's hair, all that burnished copper with auburn and gold highlights—compliments of the sun—needed a trim, but that didn't stop Mason's hands from itching to run their fingers through the shaggy mop.

Soren's mouth, Mason mused, was too wide for his narrow face, but a man could lay his claim there. Mason wanted to. He felt movement behind his zipper and ground his teeth. He most definitely had a concussion; something must have been knocked loose. His good judgment most likely. Why else would his only thought be of Soren's mouth?

Soren's jade green eyes opened. He blinked and the flutter of his golden lashes released Mason from his stare. Still, he couldn't bring himself to move away.

"Blue Heaven Motel?" he rasped.

"Yeah. You don't remember?"

"Vaguely."

Soren propped himself up on his elbow and touched fingers to the bandage covering Mason's side. "Ben called someone and she came and stitched you up."

"The Sprite?"

"With the port authority. Your brother's out there, taking care of things." Soren explained how Stoney and Ben had agreed it would be safer not to return The Sprite to her home berth at the Agat Small Boat Harbor. Stoney had flashed his badge and Mason's yacht had been granted temporary refuge among the smaller fishing ships at the Port Authority on Cabras Island, Guam's only commercial port.

Mason nodded. Stoney could buy them a few hours with law enforcement, but they'd have to go in eventually. His eyes strayed to Soren's wide mouth again. Before he knew what he was doing, he leaned forward and kissed Soren.

He didn't have the chance to do more than brush his lips across Soren's as just then the door to the bathroom opened and Ben appeared in a billowing cloud of soap-scented steam. He must have seen, because there was an edge to his voice when he needlessly announced, "I'm done."

Mason groaned and swore under his breath. The primal pulse across his groin suddenly echoed inside his skull and the metallic taste of nausea bloomed over his tongue. He dropped his head back on the pillow, but thought he caught Soren's smile before the redhead rolled out of bed and snatched up his discarded T-shirt.

"Well, you're not dying, I guess," Ben said, crossing his arms over his bare chest, giving Mason a dark look and Soren just enough room to slip into the bathroom. "Hormones seem to work just fine."

Mason winced.

"I'm chalking this up to a head wound and blood loss," he continued very evenly, which was in stark contrast to the fierce scowl he directed at Mason prone on the bed. "That was the most unprofessional thing I've seen you do since, oh, I don't know when."

Like all human beings, Mason was prone to the occasional mistake. His bigger mistakes seemed to happen in intervals of five years: his farce of a marriage at age eighteen, the divorce at twenty-three, slugging a superior officer in the Army at a supposedly mature twenty-eight and now Soren.

The shower started running and Mason dared one longing look over Ben's shoulder at the bathroom door.

"—and start thinking with your head."

Mason didn't have the heart or chance to tell his partner he'd only caught the very end of his lecture. The room door was suddenly thrown wide open. Stoney, balancing a tray with cups and several take-out bags waltzed in, announcing, "I've got coffee, burgers and aspirin. Yo, bro. How's the head?"

"His motor functions are back, but his wits haven't quite made it."

Stoney laughed. "Something happen?"

Soren didn't catch Ben's answer. He had his ear pressed against the door, but Stoney's rumbling laugh and the noise of the shower drowned out Ben's explanation. And here he'd thought Ben liked him.

"Let's talk while Red's in the shower," Stoney said, passing by the bathroom door, "The kid's trouble, Mason."

Soren rolled his eyes. But at least he'd known that Stoney wasn't a fan of his.

"Don't start. I'm not buying the terrorist theory."

"Oh yeah? He filled us in while you were out. Got tangled up with a chick named Jolina who's got a thing for kidnapping U.S. citizens."

"Kaoru—"

"Kaoru pawned Red off on you, because he needed a reliable babysitter until he could get around to looking into his story. Trust me, it's not on the top of his list. Red wasn't telling him anything new. I did some quick checking and apparently this kidnapping for ransom business is an accepted everyday business practice for thugs in the Philippines."

There was a long pause that had Soren straining to hear anything. He wished he could turn the shower off.

"Here's the thing," Stoney continued. His voice sounded oddly muffled. Soren suspected he was chewing on his burger. His own stomach cramped in protest. He wouldn't have minded something to eat and a cup of coffee. He wouldn't have minded being included in this conversation. Hell, that was his life they were discussing.

"You've got some thugs in the Philippines going about their business, big deal. You've got The Smile right under your nose and his son willing to chit-chat. If you were Kaoru, who'd you be more likely to go after?"

Soren's stomach dropped. He stepped away from the door. No, he'd made it very clear; his father's business was a non-negotiable item. If the feds wanted to get their hands on James they'd have to do it without Soren's help.

Soren yanked a hand through his hair and stared at his foggy mirror image with wide eyes. His father had been right, he mused bitterly. He was a gullible fool. Kaoru hadn't stashed him with Mason out of the goodness of his heart. He'd wanted something in return.

Mason said something Soren didn't hear. Reluctantly, he stepped up to the door again. He wasn't so sure he wanted to hear the rest of this.

"Yeah, possibly," Stoney agreed. "I'm willing to bet Kaoru has eyes and ears on The Smile. But he didn't bother telling you that Jolina, the terrorista, is in country, did he?"

The last of Soren's appetite fled.

"She has been for a few days now. I checked with my buddy at immigration. My money's on her. That chick taking a chunk out of your hide, I'm willing to bet she wasn't working for The Smile."

"Soren?"

Soren cringed.

"Didn't seem to think it was his father after him. But I wouldn't expect him to say so if he did. He's not ready to give up dear old dad yet. He's had loyalty beaten into him."

Soren felt the weight of his lies and secrets dragging at him. He sank on the toilet, staring down at his bare toes. He shouldn't have eavesdropped. He should have taken that shower. He could have walked out there, had his burger and maybe a quick moment to tell Mason he hadn't minded the kiss, would in fact like to kiss again.

His father had had that right, too. He was willing to follow where his hormones led him, and they were neither good judges of character nor too discriminating, apparently.

Angry with himself and his circumstances, Soren shot to his feet. He had to leave. He couldn't stay here. He'd already gotten Mason hurt. The man had barely escaped with his life and right now, thanks to Soren's continued silence on the matter, he woefully underestimated the danger he was in.

That Jolina was on Guam complicated the matter, but Soren didn't think he had much to fear from her right now. Even if she knew he'd turned her in, she had no idea where he was and she wasn't likely to find out in time.

A plan in mind, Soren opened the small bathroom window and climbed through. He dropped in the access alley behind the motel and scared a scrawny cat who ducked hissing behind a banged-up trash can.

He'd go home. Running into his father wasn't an issue. It was a weekday; the man was at the office. He needed to pack a few things; he could hardly show up at the airport in bloody shorts, an oversized shirt and bare feet. He needed his passports—thanks to his mother, he was a Swedish citizen as well as an American—some cash and the first flight off the island. He'd go to his grandparents. He had no idea if Sweden had any kind of extradition agreement with the United States or if he'd be of any interest to Kaoru and the FBI at all after he left. He'd given Stoney his statement. Mason's brother had made him write it down. That should cover it, he figured.

Staying ahead of Mason and, more importantly, his brother shouldn't be that difficult. They couldn't do much more than drive by his house, maybe send a patrol car to check. They'd hardly call James, and they certainly wouldn't stake out the airport.

Soren jogged down the alley, feeling guilty. He knew Mason would come after him. The man took his responsibilities seriously, but right now he could barely see straight and that would slow him down.

13

"**W**hat?" James slapped the palms of his hands on the polished surface of his massive desk and surged to his feet.

His security specialist, one Carl Cruz, a tall gangly man with a bruised forehead, shrank back.

James could not believe it. The FBI was snooping around. Lauro Miciano was sweating; his niece was asking for Soren. And his own people sabotaged him with this botched attempt, this asinine stunt, of returning Soren. It was not just the overkill and subsequent failure that pissed James off, but the utter stupidity behind it.

His temper riled, James stalked up to the bar, dropped ice

cubes into a crystal tumbler and poured himself some imported water. Stomach acid was eating away at his esophagus. Frustration and ulcers would give him cancer one day.

"Did she have any I.D. on her?"

"No, sir."

"Your cousin?"

"Yes, sir."

James thought of Jolina and her terrorist cousins. What was it with cousins? While he could appreciate families working together, James did not think handing out work assignments to any old blood relative was a prudent move. He was fairly sure Cruz could have found a better qualified criminal in a different branch of his family tree.

"And you are certain that Soren, not this Mason character, shot her?"

"Yes, sir."

Good for him. These bumbling idiots deserved to have their asses handed to them by his son. "How the hell did 'find Soren and bring him back' turn into a shootout? If I wanted my son kidnapped at gunpoint, I would have said so. Did I?"

Carl stammered out explanations and excuses, but James did not listen. This was of course the price he paid for surrounding himself with professionals who were anything but. "Get out of my sight," he snapped.

Carl slunk away like a dog with his tail tucked between his legs, and James resisted the urge to snatch the heavy glass urn off his table and hurl it after the man. It would probably kill the idiot and his blood would ruin the Turkish Hereie carpet. It was an impressive hand-knotted silk carpet with gold thread—the Rolls Royce of silk carpets—and well insured, but James did not feel like explaining to the authorities how his hired help had slipped, fallen and cracked his head open. He was already explaining too much and he abhorred explaining himself.

James was not a man to skirt the truth. He knew it was his fault Soren was quickly becoming a temperamental and willful heir. His son was spoiled, lazy and selfish. But he could not blame the boy. Soren was a product of James's misguided attempt to let the boy find his own way. He had been too lenient as a father, overlooked too much. Like a fool, he had allowed Soren to indulge his silly interest in woodworking. Two years he had patiently waited for Soren to return to the family and his responsibilities here. Allowing him this luxury, though, to go off and do his own thing, without regard for the family, had been a mistake. The boy was filled now with a sense of entitlement. And James had no one to blame but himself.

No sooner had James finished his thought than his private line rang. He sighed. He knew who it was, and he did not need her to contact the authorities to file a missing person's report, which she threatened to do and which she was perfectly capable of doing if pushed.

Downing water in angry gulps, James returned to his desk.

"Caren."

"Our son, where is he, James? He still hasn't called." She was upset. He could tell. The vein crossing his temple started throbbing.

Of his ex-wives, Caren had always been and still was the sexiest. Her late forties were extremely good to her. She was in great shape and quite possibly more beautiful now than she had been in her twenties when he had met her at some benefit gala in Tokyo. He had instantly fallen in love with her scarlet tresses and her flawless, porcelain complexion. After a whirlwind courtship he had brought her back to Guam.

"I'm at home," she said and the way she said it told James she was not talking about her sprawling Boston condo, but her childhood home outside Malmö, Sweden.

She had been a minor celebrity on Guam, but in her homeland, she was an icon. She had her own skin care line—100% natural, not tested on animals—and specialty cosmetics for redheads. After her divorce from James, she had been rumored to have had an affair with someone associated with the Swedish royal family, some distant cousin (always cousins) no closer to the throne than the lay person on the street.

Even after nearly twenty years, the thought alone made James jealous and his stomach churn.

"I want Soren to join us." Us. Her family. James had met his in-laws once. The dislike had been instant and mutual. He cringed and rubbed his forehead.

"I want him on the plane by the end of the week. Do you think you can do that, James?"

James exhaled slowly and pressed his fingers against his throbbing temple. He needed more water.

"I called the house," she continued. "I spoke to Danielle yesterday. Soren hasn't been home in a week, she said. Where is my son, James? What have you done to him? Is there something going on?"

James snorted. He would wring Soren's neck for not calling his mother. How difficult could it have been to call? Surely this Mason character must have had a phone on his boat.

"I swear, James, if you did something to him, I—"

"You what?" James snapped, temper riled. He took a deep breath and tried again, "Caren?"

"I called the police, James."

Of course she had. James ground his teeth. "Did you know your son has been dating a woman suspected of terrorism?" He did not think Jolina and her cohorts were more than thugs kidnapping for ransom, but these days every second-rate loon with a grudge against the United States was a terrorist. He did not even think Jolina's family had anything against the U.S. They sure liked the money coming in. "I told him to be careful," he said, infusing his voice with fatherly concern. "In fact, we argued about it. I warned him not to piss off that girl's uncle. But you know how he listens to me."

James's exact words, as a matter of fact, had been, 'If she complains again that you are not receptive to her charms, you will regret coming home.' That constituted warning as far as James was concerned.

"You don't think something happened to him, do you?"

James thought of Carl Cruz being forced to abandon his dead cousin at gun point. "I am certain he is fine. Trust me, Caren, honey." He smiled. She might have been a nuisance, but unlike the other mothers of his children, she did not live off her monthly alimony. She was a successful and shrewd businesswoman in her own right, and he respected her for that. And it did not hurt that she remained the sexiest woman he knew. So he forgave her the annoying phone calls and threats and her impulsive mothering instincts. "Right now, nothing would please me more than to put our son"—he emphasized the words—"on a plane to get rid of him."

"Maybe he could—"

"We had an agreement, Caren." It was the same agreement he had with his other ex-wives. They received money, jewels, houses and whatever else they wished, like their daughters. He kept his sons. Well, and Danielle, but that was a whole other story and not one he enjoyed remembering. "I do not care if he visits. I never meant to keep him from his grandparents"—he knew what they were saying about him—"but after this blows over, he will have to come back. There is work waiting for him here."

"All right," she sighed. "You won't do anything rash? James?"

"Of course not," he assured her and severed the connection. Soren would wish for rashness, he vowed. After a week of irritating phone calls and Lauro Miciano pacing his office, brow sweaty, worried about the feds snooping into his business, James figured nothing he might do to Soren could be construed as rash or impulsive.

But if Caren wanted her son on a plane by the end of the week, then finding him became even more imperative. She would just have to wait a few extra days, James figured.

He glanced at the watch circling his wrist and activated his intercom. "Get me Lieutenant Gray," he barked at his secretary.

Gray was not only precinct commander but father of five college-age children and a lover of cockfights and dog races. James happily financed the education of Gray's daughters and his gambling habit in exchange for the occasional favor.

This Mason character—born Brook Mason Ward, second

son to a working-class family, according to James's information—who had butted into Buchanan family business was in all likelihood still explaining to some desk cop the night invasion on his boat that had ended with considerable bloodshed.

Gray would find both the cop taking the report and the man giving it. He would take care of things, including Caren's official missing person's report.

Of course, James would offer to take care of the damages his idiotic security personnel had caused. In his experience, very large and very impressive checks generally smoothed any rough waters, and a man of Mason's caliber and connections should not be left wanting or holding grudges. He would forget about Soren and disappear. That was understood.

"Gray?" James lifted the receiver to his ear. It was early still, with any luck this could be taken care of before lunch.

14

Hitchhikers were virtually unheard of on Guam, which was why Soren figured luck was on his side. The very first car he flagged down stopped for him. A good omen for sure.

He made it to Mangilao in record time. His spare key was still where he'd hidden it in the backyard and his father hadn't thought to change the locks (and why would he?). His teenage half-sister Danielle—fourth marriage progeny—shouldn't have been at home, a small wrinkle in his plan, but since she wasn't willing to admit to cutting school, she wasn't going to call their father to inform him of Soren's return. So far, so good.

If his luck held, the people with vested interest in him

wouldn't think he'd return home and his credit card would have enough credit left to get him a ticket off the island. Oh, and Danielle would stop dogging his every step. As it was, she kept following him through the house and didn't hesitate at all at the threshold to his room. She sidestepped the T-shirt he'd dropped and flung herself on his unmade bed.

"Where have you been? Why didn't you call? What kind of trouble are you in? You're not going to tell Dad I was home, are you? Is that blood? Whose clothes are you wearing? Hey, your mom called for you. Jolina, too. What the hell is going on? Why are you packing? Where are you going? Hello, I'm talking to you."

Soren sighed. He knew from experience that ignoring her didn't work. She'd keep up her end of the conversation until he acknowledged her. He stopped stuffing his backpack with clothes and turned to face his sister. "Danny—"

"Soren," she mocked in a very good, much put upon imitation of her brother. "You're not, like, in trouble with the police, are you?"

"No." Not that he knew of. "I'm in trouble with Dad, and I'm not going to rat you out, if you're going to forget you saw me. Deal?"

"You bet."

"Can you do me a huge favor?"

Her eyes narrowed. "I'm broke," she informed him, crossing her arms under her breasts.

Soren shook his head. He had a small stash of emergency cash hidden away and he was fairly sure she did, too. Life with their father required a certain amount of preparedness.

"I was thinking food. Can you microwave something for me?"

Danielle gaped at him.

He flashed her a wide smile and a quick "Thanks," before he slammed the bathroom door in her face and started the shower. His plan to get out of Dodge started washing down the drain along with two days worth of sweat and the suds of organic peppermint shampoo.

Exhaustion caught up with him under the warm spray.

And with it memories of Mason crumpling against the galley counter, the Filipina's body jerking with the impact of the first bullet, the feel of her gun recoiling in his hand. He stayed in the shower until his stomach stopped heaving and the water turned cold.

Weary and entirely ready to leave his troubles behind—okay, run away again—he emerged from the bathroom only to be confronted by the ruins of his plan.

"Hey, babe."

He wouldn't have been more surprised had Mason lounged on his bed, a bottle of Pepsi in his large hand. "Hi," he croaked. Where the hell had she come from?

"You know, I had to bribe Danny to call me the exact second you came home. Where have you been? You okay, baby? You look tired." Jolina patted the spot next to her on his bed. "Come. Lay down."

She looked good propped up against his headboard. She wore her long black hair swept up and not much else. The lacy fabric of her matching bra and panties did very little to cover her. If she was going to confront him about his betrayal, she wasn't going to do it fully clothed.

Unable to come up with a good excuse not to, Soren stretched out on his bed next to her. She tsked at him and coaxed him on his stomach. "So tense," she murmured. "Relax, baby."

She curled her small hand around his ankle. Her thumb traced the scar he had there from a skateboarding accident a decade ago. Then, lightly scraping a red nail over his skin, her hand traveled upwards. Over his calf, and he exhaled. Over the back of his knee, and he inhaled slowly. Over the back of his thigh, and he held his breath.

"Hmm," she murmured, crawling up on the bed beside him. "So sensitive," she whispered between his shoulder blades and flattened her hand across his thigh. "Right here." She pushed her hand under the edge of his towel and her red nails scraped the swell of his buttock.

Instantly, without fail, he came to attention. Nowhere—save one very intimate zone—was his skin as responsive to touch as it was across the back of his legs. But there was no heat backing up his body's reaction to her touch.

"I'm tired," he mumbled, not bothering to turn over or look up. The truth was he had no desire to spend any amount of time with Jolina. It surprised him a bit, this lack of desire. Jolina was every bit as addictive as the drugs she pushed on him.

"I brought gifts," she said and withdrew her hand. Soren knew what that meant. He didn't have to turn his head or even open his eyes. Getting drunk with Jolina suddenly seemed like a good idea (despite the obvious danger associated with it; this was the woman he'd betrayed to the FBI). They'd drink, have sex, she'd leave, and he'd be able to still make the airport in time to get off the island before night fall.

"Champagne," Jolina said, uncorking the bottle without the pop and spraying froth the movies had made synonymous with opening champagne bottles.

Soren did turn then, watching her drink the bubbly liquid directly from the bottle. It never ceased to amaze him how a small thing like Jolina—she was five foot two and three quarters of an inch, barely weighed a hundred pounds—could be such a powerhouse.

She nudged him with her knee and his eyes fell on the other present she'd brought with her: pills. Little reddish-orange Burmese methamphetamine and caffeine tablets. Not his preferred choice of drug, but exactly what he needed right now. He'd have to watch the talking he was prone to after a hit, but the methamphetamine would zap his fatigue and the extra energy and alertness would come in handy. Maybe her stopping by wasn't such a bad thing after all.

15

No sooner had James heard from Lieutenant Gray than his secretary's voice drifted out of the intercom. "There is a Mr. Ward here to see you."

James grinned. This should be interesting. Gray had warned him that Stone Ward might show up. Not only had the man filed the necessary reports having to do with the ambush on his brother's boat—complete with Soren's handwritten account of the shooting—but he had been informed of Caren's missing persons report as well.

"Send him in."

James did not get up nor did he extend his hand to his visitor. Instead he leaned back in his leather chair, patiently folded his hands and took measure of the man approaching his desk.

Tall. Early thirties. Brunet. The sleeves of his Hawaiian shirt stretched over bulging arms. Not the least bit intimidated and entirely aware of James taxing him.

James smoothed his trademark smile into place and displayed the perfect blend of curiosity and boredom. "What is it that I can do for you today?"

Stone flipped open his wallet, displaying his badge. "Guam Police Department. Stone Ward," he said. "I am trying to find your son, Mr. Buchanan." Unbidden, he dropped into a chair before the massive desk and got comfortable.

"I am sorry, but you are going to have to be more precise, Mr. Ward. I have three sons. That I know of." James grinned. He enjoyed giving the impression that there were more than three of them. To forestall Ward's answer James held up his hand in a practiced gesture. "I think I can guess. My youngest is a bit of a troublemaker."

"Is he?"

James managed a thoughtful expression and rubbed his chin. "Are you a father, Mr. Ward? You see, even when they outgrow their teenage years, some of them, how shall I say, remain rebellious and difficult to control."

"And what is it you do to bring them back under control?"

James did not let the barb faze him. He had all the advantages in this conversation, and he was not going to let Ward rile him. "If it is Soren you are looking for, I must disappoint you. He is not here." He gestured at the offices outside his suite. "He has an office waiting for him here, but I am afraid he is not interested in carrying on the family tradition." He pushed his brows into a frown. "He has not been at home either. For several days now. As a matter of fact, I just spoke to his mother on the phone. She is worried."

"Does she have reason to be?"

"I am an influential businessman, Mr. Ward. I have had a long and very successful career. As much as it galls me, I have enemies." He paused thoughtfully, forehead still creased, letting Stoney sort out the implications of that statement.

"Unlike his mother, you don't seem too concerned about your son's absence."

James nodded. "As you probably know, my firm has attracted some unfair attention recently. I have been very busy and distracted lately, I admit, but Soren is a grown man who can come and go as he chooses."

"Does he often disappear for days on end?"

"I would hardly call it 'disappearing' when he stays with one of his ever-changing, new friends for several days. Like I said, he is a grown man and not required to check in with me."

James took a slow glance at his wristwatch and leaned forward in his chair. He straightened the file in front of him—Stone Daniel Ward's dossier, incidentally—before fastening his eyes on the older twin arrogantly slouching in his chair.

"Now, what is it that you want, Mr. Ward? As I said, I am a very busy man, and I do not think you have come here looking for Soren." He leaned back again, tapping a long finger against his full bottom lip, and played his ace. "Unless your brother, in whose company he has spent these last few days, if my information is correct, has lost him."

James had hoped for some reaction, some show of confusion perhaps, but Ward had commendable control over his features. He nodded, looked thoughtful, but did not appear surprised. James knew he had made a mistake.

"You didn't tell your ex-wife you knew where Soren was."

"Mr. Ward," James said, voice a few degrees cooler, smile gone. He should not have let Ward goad him into shooting his mouth off. "What I did or did not tell Caren is none of your business. Let me tell you this. I am a very wealthy businessman. If I wanted my son returned to me, I would have contacted your brother and offered a substantial amount of money for Soren's return. Until several hours ago, I had no need to spend the effort or money." He smoothed his smile back into place, though it was more difficult now than it had been at the onset of their conversation. "As we both know, Caren needs to speak to her son, so I am prepared to pay handsomely to have him back home. Today."

Stoney nodded. Yes, he understood. Buchanan's ex-wife was worried about Soren's safety. She knew what his father was capable of; she'd lived with the man. Really, The Smile's temper was a badly kept secret. "Do you hit him?"

James's short bark of laughter had nothing to do with amusement. "You are an officer of the law, you cannot expect me to answer that question. But I will tell you this, Soren has a way of testing my limits and overstepping his bounds. As do you."

Stone broke out in a wide grin. "Because I am an officer of the law, I know that was not a threat, Mr. Buchanan, or was it?"

"Of course not. Now, if you will excuse me. I do have work to do." James did get to his feet then. "Please pass my offer along to your brother. I do not know how he got involved in this"—that was a blatant lie, James knew full well the FBI had called in Mason—"but, as I said, I need to see my son returned to me, and I am willing to offer a reward for his return. A substantial reward a man of your brother's caliber can appreciate."

He waited until the door closed behind Stone Ward to surge to his feet and pace his office. Soren's statement, which Gray had faxed over, did not identify Cruz or his position in the Buchanan hierarchy of employees. But had he told Stone Ward what he knew? Had Stone Ward come to fish for information or to alert James to their involvement? No, the man was not stupid and Soren had obviously shot his mouth off about family matters. The Wards knew James was behind that asinine stunt, and the cop had come to let him know he was not going to do anything about it. Money it was then.

James strode back to his desk. He had made his offer. They would probably let the afternoon drag on before contacting him, an annoying byproduct of these kinds of negotiations, but one he was willing to overlook as long as he got his hands on Soren before the day was done.

16

"Here we are," Ben said as he pulled his car up in front of the Buchanan property at the end of an exclusive cul-de-sac, a stone's throw from the University of Guam campus. On a large piece of land that hugged the Mangilao cliff line, the two-story sprawling Spanish-style villa nestled among lush landscaping that hid it from curious views and kept the unrelenting, year-round sun at bay. Hedges, leafy greenery, and bougainvilleas in a riot of vibrant colors camouflaged the six-foot wall surrounding the property. The circular driveway was private and gated. "Nice place."

Mason scowled. He was still replaying the phone conversation he'd just had with Stoney. His brother's "dumb fuck" and "shit for brains" rankled. Probably more so because he knew his twin was right. He gingerly massaged his throbbing temple. He should have stayed in bed, should have let Stoney and Ben track down Soren. But Stoney and Ben hadn't been hired to keep Soren safe.

"What did Stoney have to say?"

Mason clenched his jaw. "Buchanan's a slick bastard and I'm a dumbass."

Ben mumbled something under his breath that sounded suspiciously like he agreed with Stoney's character assessment. Mason dragged a hand across the stubble on his jaw and groaned.

Contrary to their very vocal opinions about his understanding of the situation, he got it. They were concerned, and they had reason to be. His head hurt like hell, and he was low on blood. If push came to shove, he would stumble. What they didn't understand was that while they worried about him, no one worried about Soren. Oh, sure, they wanted to find him, too; Stoney, because his witness was AWOL and his job was on the line, and Ben, because Mason's professional reputation reflected on Security Solutions.

The truth was, Mason cared about Soren.

"I'm so going to kick his ass," he murmured and caught Ben's slanted look. His friend didn't seem to think kicking was what was on his mind.

"You're sure about this?"

Mason nodded. His internal clock was off by hours, but according to Ben's dashboard clock it was mid-afternoon, which meant Soren had had plenty of time to return home. The officer Stoney had sent to check on things after he'd learned of the missing persons report had rung the doorbell and walked the sprawling property, noting nothing out of place. But Mason wasn't satisfied with the man's report. If Soren was home, he wouldn't have been foolish enough to open the door.

Mason was determined to break and enter to make sure Soren wasn't hiding out inside. He stepped into the oppressing humidity of early September and clipped his radio to the waistband of his jeans. He slid his earpiece into place and pulled its coiled cord under his T-shirt, connecting it to the radio. The casual onlooker wouldn't notice he was wired. Ben tested the mike on his radio, his voice loud and clear in Mason's left ear. Mason nodded at his partner and set off for the gate across the street.

The gate, more deterrent than actual obstacle, was unlocked, which had Mason grumbling about proper lack of security. As he approached the house, gravel crunching under his boots, he saw a red sedan parked around the side of the villa and figured he'd just knock on the front door for starters. He dropped the heavy brass knocker twice and waited.

The teenager who opened the door gave him a thorough once-over, then raised perfectly plucked eyebrows and the corners of her mouth. "Yes?"

"Hi. I'm looking for—"over the girl's shoulder he saw Soren step off the sweeping stairs—"him."

Her smile widened as she pushed the door open for him without any apparent concern for her brother's or her own safety. He would have expected The Smile's kids to have more security savvy. The man's wealth and prominent position among Guam's elite had to make his children prime kidnapping candidates. Then again, the local lowlife probably knew better than to mess with The Smile.

He stepped into an entry hall so highly polished and gleaming that he had to fight the instinct to take his shoes off.

"Is he in trouble?" the girl asked with the kind of sibling glee Mason recognized.

"Yes."

She grinned and he glowered. "Nice place," he said.

She shrugged. "Yeah, I guess."

Nice was an understatement, of course. Soaring ceilings, tall windows, hardwood floors—only the best for The Smile and his family. Mason passed plenty of leather in a formal living room and a large dining room that probably required a dinner jacket. With the girl by his side, he rounded a corner and found himself in a sprawling family room more obviously lived in. Floor-to-ceiling windows took full advantage of the villa's cliffside perch and panoramic waterfront exposure. He whistled appreciatively, then headed after Soren, calling out the redhead's name.

"Not now," Soren spat over his bare shoulder and across the den. "Now's really not a good time."

"Now," Mason insisted loudly just as someone slammed the swinging kitchen door open and Soren had to jump back to avoid having his head bashed in.

"I should shoot you and be done with it." The brunette was spitting mad. "Son of a bitch. Why did you come back? Do you know what they do to people they—Did you tell anyone about what happened?"

"Lover's quarrel," the teenager at Mason's side helpfully stage-whispered to him.

Soren hung his head and groaned. Jolina's dark eyes homed in on the girl like lasers, before taking Mason's measure in one long, hard stare. "Who the hell are you?"

"Mason. And you are?" He knew who she was. The terrorista. Stoney and Ben had filled him in on her.

"Mason? You are Mason?"

He didn't like the way her eyes lit up or Soren cringed away from her. Adrenaline rushed through his system.

"This is the guy?"

He had the sneaking suspicion his name might not have come up during polite conversation. Not judging by the disbelief written all over her pretty features or Soren's acute discomfort and his tousled, half-naked state.

"This is the guy you think of while I suck your dick?"

Mason moved to Soren's side, close enough to get a whiff of booze. He growled low in his throat and his hand clamped like a vice around Soren's elbow.

The redhead blushed fiercely. "Jo," he pleaded.

"Don't Jo me," she said. "Why don't you take him upstairs. Maybe he'll fuck you." Her dark head swiveled in Mason's direction as she sized him up. There was nothing wholesome or healthy about the smile that followed her look. "You don't seem like a guy who takes it up the ass." She jerked her chin in Soren's direction. "He does. Well, his ass is all yours."

Soren blushed an even darker shade of crimson. His sister giggled. Mason felt lightheaded as his hormones flooded already adrenaline-saturated blood.

"You heard the lady, let's go." He steered Soren toward the still swinging kitchen door.

"I—"

"Not now." Mason transferred his grip to Soren's neck and pushed him toward the door. He stabbed a finger at the teenager. "Disappear," he advised. "Call 911 if you hear shots."

"This is too cool." Soren's sister trotted off.

The telltale sound of a slide being pulled back on a semi-automatic stopped Mason. Shit. He turned and stepped in front of Soren, shielding him from Jolina's anger and the bullet he felt her completely capable of firing. He tuned out Ben's voice in his left ear—two Filipinos in their late twenties approaching the front door—and concentrated on Jolina. She kept her gun aimed squarely at his chest and her beautiful dark eyes on him. She didn't smile. "Who are you?"

Mason knew she wasn't asking his name. She'd heard it; she knew it. He remained quiet.

Her lips thinned with annoyance.

There was no doubt in Mason's mind that even with a hole in his head and his world constantly swaying under his feet—it was almost like the gently rocking motion of the Sprite—he could physically overpower the petite woman. But only a fool would rush someone with a weapon at the ready.

"He's mine now," he tipped his head in Soren's direction, "and I mean to keep it that way." He kept his language deliberately vague and his gaze intent. Then the realization nearly made him flinch as his words sank in. Maybe it was saying those words out loud, but suddenly he knew that was exactly what he intended to do: keep Soren for himself.

"Hey, I—"

"Shut up, Soren." Jolina jerked her eyes over Mason's shoulder to the redhead, but the gun didn't waver. Her dark eyes bored into Soren and the message was clear. She was still a woman who'd heard her lover call out someone else's name and the redhead knew better than to challenge her.

Her eyes flicked back to Mason. She tilted her head, her dark look grazing his left ear and the clear wire disappearing down his shirt. "Someone's talking to you."

Mason raised his hand to his ear. "My partner."

One of the men outside dropped the heavy antique doorknocker against the front door. The noise echoed.

"That my cousins?"

Mason nodded. Ben, in his ear, suspected the arrivals were unarmed. Sandals, shorts and muscle shirts didn't lend themselves to concealing weapons.

Jolina cursed under her breath. She hitched her chin at the kitchen door. "In there," she ordered.

Soren balked. "Just shoot us already."

"Speak for yourself," Mason said.

"Not yet. Maybe later." She jabbed the barrel of the gun at the kitchen door. "Move it."

Mason was reluctant to turn his back, but controlling Soren, who wasn't nearly as calm as Jolina, outweighed keeping an eye on her and the gun. "Do as the lady says," he suggested and clamped his hand around Soren's neck again.

Mason most definitely had a concussion and no business trying to protect Soren from the threats in his life—irate terrorist girlfriends, fathers, possible others, who knew?—because while there was a gun trained on him, all his senses registered was the sliding of his thumb into Soren's hair at the nape of his neck. Hair that was still damp from a shower or the earlier exertions Jolina had mentioned so carelessly.

Soren dug in his heels and set his spine, ready to refuse cooperation, but Mason didn't give him a chance. His head was pounding and his right hand circling Soren's neck was probably bruising the redhead, but he maneuvered them into the kitchen without antagonizing Jolina further.

The kitchen, Mason noted with some envy, didn't just sport palatial dimensions, granite counters, two center islands, top-tier amenities and a cozy dining area, but a stunning garden view. A man could entertain here.

"You're a freaking idiot, Soren. You should have just

stayed lost."

Mason silently agreed with her.

She pointed at a heavy door that looked like it led to a basement. "Open it."

Soren didn't budge. He crossed his arms in front of his chest and challenged Jolina with a dark look.

Mason suppressed a smile. That was the Soren he knew. Obstinate and difficult. Soren was either stupid or fearless. Mason suspected it was a combination of both, brought on by the consumption of alcohol.

Jolina smiled and for a moment her eyes connected with Mason's, then they lost their warmth. When she addressed Soren, there was a wealth of warning in her voice. "We've had some great times, baby. I like you. But if I have to, I will shoot you."

"What's stopping you?"

She shrugged. "I like you. I really do." Her gaze slid down Soren's smooth chest to the precariously clinging jeans, still unbuttoned. "I'm not willing to give you up just yet."

She nodded at the door again. "You know what they do. You know what happens if I let them in and they find you here. Why the fuck did you come back? Did you tell anyone about what happened? I vouched for you, Soren. Do you know what that means? Someone's been talking to the feds. They know shit."

Jolina's voice rose with each question and Soren must have decided that her anger had reached the boiling point. He opened the heavy door to a dark room and stepped inside.

Jolina waved her gun at Mason. "The earpiece. The radio. Leave it."

Mason reluctantly did as he was told, then followed Soren into what he assumed to be a safe room, designed to protect the family during typhoons. The door fell shut. The sound of the locking mechanism as Jolina turned the key was ominous in the dark. Her voice reached past the heavy barrier. "Make no mistake, Soren," she said. "If it was you snitching to the feds, I'll shoot you myself."

"Not if I wring his neck first," Mason grumbled.

17

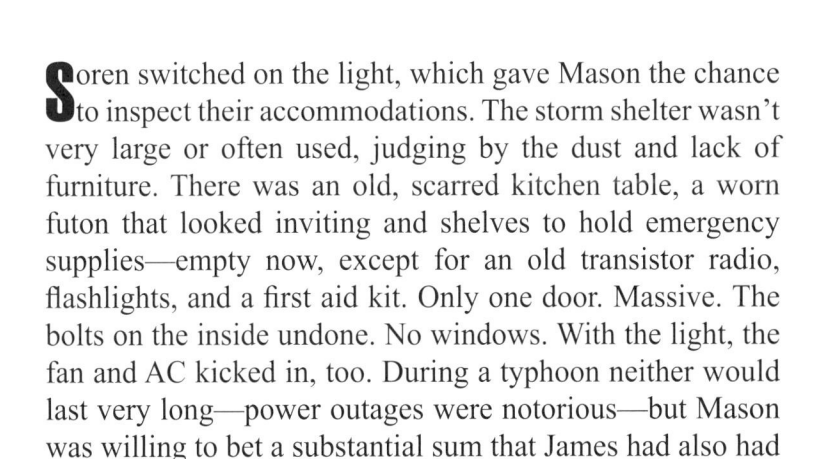

Soren switched on the light, which gave Mason the chance to inspect their accommodations. The storm shelter wasn't very large or often used, judging by the dust and lack of furniture. There was an old, scarred kitchen table, a worn futon that looked inviting and shelves to hold emergency supplies—empty now, except for an old transistor radio, flashlights, and a first aid kit. Only one door. Massive. The bolts on the inside undone. No windows. With the light, the fan and AC kicked in, too. During a typhoon neither would last very long—power outages were notorious—but Mason was willing to bet a substantial sum that James had also had an emergency generator installed, which, like the room itself, probably hadn't been used since Typhoon Pongsona devastated the island in 2002.

Resigned to his fate, his brain throbbing and pounding inside his skull, Mason sank onto the futon. He scrubbed a hand over his face and tried his best to ignore Soren.

"You okay? You don't look so hot. Should you be up? Honestly, I didn't think you'd be up."

He speared Soren with a contemptuous look. "You're high."

Soren's dilated pupils spoke for themselves. He didn't bother denying the truth. He paced the length of the storm room, fidgeted with the radio, paced to the other side.

Mason massaged his right temple before anger drove him to his feet. "What the fuck were you thinking? What, you'd just go back home like all those other times, get drunk, and that would be the end of that? Maybe let your father beat the crap out of you again tomorrow, when you're sober? Is that it? Make up with what's her name and pretend her people didn't just board my boat! God damn you, Soren."

"Oh, screw you. That wasn't my plan at all. I was trying to get the hell out of here."

"Yeah, sure you were. For someone who isn't stupid, you're a dumb son of a bitch, Soren. You're the most confrontational and belligerent—" Mason snapped his mouth shut and yanked a hand through his hair, pulling on the stitches underneath. Arguing with Soren wouldn't get him anywhere. He took a deep breath. Exhaled slowly, and tried again, "You're so busy fighting everyone off, you can't see the people fighting for you."

"What the fuck is that supposed to mean?"

"That means I'm on your side, and it's high time you were on your side, too."

"Fuck."

Mason swallowed a groan. He couldn't help it. His eyes were already cataloguing all the details. Soren's smooth, hairless chest, liberally dusted with freckles. His small, pale nipples. The soft hair that surrounded his navel and grew downward to become his pubic hair, a shade darker than the coppery strands that always hung in his face and obscured his green eyes. Soren hadn't fastened the buttons to his jeans and there wasn't much left to the imagination there.

With some effort, Mason dragged his eyes away from Soren's crotch. His gaze dropped further and slid over Soren's bare feet, noting the way Soren's jeans broke over his arches. He stared transfixed. Like the rest of the redhead, Soren's feet were lean and elegantly cut. His toes begged to be massaged. Mason shifted his weight to ease the pressure behind his zipper.

Soren stopped pacing to stare at Mason. "Why don't you get us the hell out of here?"

"What do you want me to do?"

"Put your shoulder to the door? I don't know. Aren't you supposed to be some security hotshot?"

The thought alone made Mason wince. He fingered the lump on his head and groaned. He'd known from the moment they met that the redhead would be one big killer headache. He should have stayed in bed. But no, he couldn't have let Stoney and Ben track Soren down. Damn sense of responsibility.

Soren smirked and resumed his pacing. "Got some painkillers upstairs."

"Wiseass." Mason propped his hip against the edge of the table. Soren's restless movements were making him dizzy.

"I bet you flunked out of bodyguard school. You're not very good at it."

Mason felt his anger rising once more and closed his eyes in an effort to calm himself. No one ever won an argument with a drunk, he told himself.

"I saw you fight on the Sprite. Why didn't you just grab Jolina? You know, some fancy karate action, flip her on her back or something?"

Mason stood abruptly and with two quick strides had Soren cornered. "What are you doing here? Were you running away from me?"

Soren's chin rose. His jade eyes flashed green fire. He opened his mouth, probably to hurl curses and obscenities at

Mason. But Mason covered that mouth with his, devouring the startled protest. His fingers bit into Soren's bare arms. He felt the redhead tremble against his body and pulled back.

But Soren's mouth followed him, eagerly kissing back. Mason's hands slid into Soren's long hair. His tongue swept into Soren's mouth, staking his territory, claiming his prize. He broke away and tipped Soren's head to the side, exposing an ear that was immediately assaulted with lips and tongue and the gentle edge of teeth. When Soren moaned, Mason chuckled and slid his hands out of the red mop and over Soren's shoulders, while his mouth followed the curve of Soren's neck.

Mason's hands skimmed down Soren's flanks until they came to rest over the swell of his jean-clad ass. Mason pulled the redhead against his groin, pressing his bulge into Soren's deliciously flat stomach.

"God, I want you."

Mason crushed his mouth down over Soren's with unerring precision. He swallowed the last of Soren's startled exclamation, thrusting his tongue into the hot depths the way his hands plunged inside the redhead's jeans. Undone buttons were no obstacle. One hand took hold of Soren's ass again, clutching the warm flesh that fit so perfectly in his palms. One hand curled around the heated erection he found. He stroked it once, twice, then turned Soren in his arms and pulled the redhead back up against his chest. The bulge of Mason's straining erection, painfully confined to his jeans, fit comfortably against the small of Soren's back. Without thinking, he pushed Soren's jeans out of the way.

Soren tensed in his arms, but didn't resist. Mason rested his chin on Soren's shoulder. He left one hand splayed across Soren's chest, feeling the redhead's frantic heartbeat under his palm. His other hand slowly slid down Soren's flat abdomen until his fingers brushed coarse pubic hair. "God, I want you," he whispered, letting his lips linger against Soren's neck.

Soren sank back into Mason's embrace and settled his head against the crook of Mason's shoulder. He clutched Mason's thighs as if afraid the man would step away and disappear. He moaned.

Mason answered in kind. The vibrations of Soren's moan traveled up his arm and down his spine, straight into his cock, which was begging to be released from its denim prison. Not yet, he thought. Not here. He didn't have protection.

"Don't stop." Soren's hand came up and his fingers entwined with Mason's. He pushed their hands down over his cock. "Don't stop."

Mason opened his hand and let his palm glide over the head of Soren's cock, before closing his fingers around it again.

Soren groaned and thrust into the fist that held him. His hand dropped away and groped for Mason's thighs behind him.

Mason tightened his hold, curling his hand around the base of Soren's cock. He stroked, squeezed, tugged, and swirled his open palm over the satiny head. He let Soren thrust and penetrate his fist. Like the rest of the redhead, which fit snugly against Mason's curves and angles, his cock was a perfect fit for Mason's large hand.

Mason kept one hand curled around Soren's cock, while the other explored Soren's inner thighs, occasionally gliding up and under Soren's balls, applying pressure there.

"Fuck me," Soren said, his voice soft.

Mason's heart skipped a beat. His breath hitched. He groaned. God, how he wanted to, but he couldn't, not here, not without protection.

"Please," Soren begged.

Mason's cock jumped. As much as he wanted to feel himself inside Soren, he knew it wasn't going to happen. "You have no idea what you're asking."

"Please," Soren pleaded, pressing back, grinding his ass against Mason's crotch.

Mason hissed. He pushed the straining bulge testing the strength of his denim down Soren's lower back until his rock hard shaft slid between Soren's cheeks, trying to give the redhead an idea of what he was asking, hoping to dissuade more begging.

"Please," Soren whispered, not the least bit intimidated. Mason continued to stroke the redhead's cock, feeling it swell in his grip. His own shaft was ready to explode. Then Soren's body tightened, and he let out a soft, guttural moan. Mason closed his eyes and clenched his jaw as he, too, came.

Mason relaxed with Soren still in his arms. Sweat plastered his shirt to his back. His jeans were beginning to stick to him in uncomfortable places, but Soren's weight felt right against him. Then there was a pounding on the door, startling them both.

"We'll catch up with you later, Soren," Jolina's voice drifted past the heavy barrier. Was that amusement coloring her voice? "Gotta go. Your father's on his way. Danny called him."

Soren surged forward and hit the door with the flat of his palm. "No. Jo? Jolina?" But there was no answer. "God damn her."

When Soren turned he wore an expression Mason hadn't seen before. He yanked his jeans up off the floor and a hand through his tousled hair. "I should probably tell you now that the people who boarded the Sprite, uh, they weren't Jolina's people."

18

Ben, parked just outside the gated Buchanan property, didn't like that his view of the villa was obscured by a wall of flowering shrubs, but knowing that all official visitors had to pass him one way or another made up for that. Unofficial visitors would have to hike up the modest cliff from the beach or cut their way through a dense patch of jungle to escape his attention. He doubted very much anyone would go to the trouble, which meant he had no problem keeping track of the comings and goings.

Just minutes after they arrived, the two Filipinos were ready to leave again. After heated gesturing and an obvious argument with a young woman looking very much like Soren's on-again, off-again girlfriend in front of the house, they sped away in their van. Jolina followed in a red sedan that had been parked out of sight.

Ben expected Mason to leave the house with a sullen Soren in tow, but neither man appeared. Thirty minutes, two phone calls to the office and a granola bar later, right around the time Ben started to worry, a high-end, late model truck and a handful of Buchanan goons, known as The Smile's personal security detail, rolled up. And that was that. No Mason. No Soren. No sounds of rapid gunfire or breaking glass either, which was always promising.

Nevertheless worried, Ben traded the air-conditioned interior of his car for the oppressive humidity of the afternoon. Half a dozen times now he'd heard the bubbly, perky young thing on the radio warn of an approaching tropical storm, but the breeze outside his car barely stirred the leaves on the banyan tree that grew on the Buchanan property.

Ben tucked his .38 Smith & Wesson under the waistband of his shorts at the small of his back and waited until the college kids at the mouth of the cul-de-sac were engrossed in their game of hoops before he approached the gate and discreetly crept across the landscaped front yard.

He was a modern Catholic with modern beliefs, but that didn't keep him from laying a hand on the trunk of the great banyan tree and bowing his head. He mumbled a quick prayer to the *taotaomo'na*, or ancestors, who resided in the old tree. Where spirits were concerned it was always better to err on the side of caution; praying never hurt.

Ben snuck past the detached four-car garage—empty except for an old, battered Jeep—and across the tiled, covered porch that swept the full length of the house, upsetting a group of plain brown skinks that fled in all directions. He peered in windows and doors, trying locks to no avail. He spotted no one hiding on the covered second floor patio or perched outside a window—just in case Mason had been forced to leave by means of an alternate route. No one was floating in the pool, and the Jacuzzi was covered. The garden shed, discreetly tucked behind a clump of dwarf palms, was dead-bolted.

The kitchen window louvers were open and laughter spilled out. Ben crept as close as he dared, peeking inside. He saw five of The Smile's men sitting around and watching a swivel TV mounted to the wall. He didn't see what was on TV, but it must have been funny. The men were obviously amused. Thankfully, they were not engaged in activities that could be harmful to Mason or Soren.

Without much else he could do, Ben continued his survey of the sprawling property and its lush, manicured garden that was testament to the money The Smile spent on landscaping and maintenance. Buchanan had even had the jungle that should have been hugging the bluff cleared, and Ben understood why. He stood in the shade of a fan palm and took a moment to enjoy the massive, panoramic view of the blue-green Pacific and, to the south, the broad Pago Bay. There had once been a Spanish village where the Pago River emptied into the bay, but a smallpox epidemic in 1856 had wiped out its inhabitants. Ben knew his great-grandfather's family had mourned lost relatives there.

After a quick look that assured him no one had fallen to his death on the rocky shore bellow, Ben called Stoney and cautiously retreated to his car. A few minutes later, Stoney angled his fire-engine-red Jeep to the curb behind Ben's sedan.

"Mason still in there?" The older Ward twin leaned into Ben's open driver side window.

"Unless he threw himself off the cliff behind the house and his body was dragged off by giant sea creatures before I had a look."

"Soren in there?"

"He might have pushed Mason off."

"I thought you said they were, uh, chummy."

Ben curled his lip and did his best to ignore the unwanted flash of memory. Hell, he'd suspected it hadn't been his partner's altruistic nature that had made Mason take the redhead in, but seeing them kiss had come as a surprise. During their partnership and even longer friendship, he'd never actually seen Mason with another man. He was just glad he hadn't showered five minutes longer. That scene could have been far more embarrassing.

"Now what?" Ben asked to distract himself from the unwanted images his brain flashed him. "I don't like that he's in there with The Smile's men."

"You see anything that would suggest he's being kept against his will?"

"No," Ben admitted grudgingly.

Stoney scratched his chin and craned his neck to get a glimpse of the house. "I could ring the doorbell and flash my badge. See what happens. But I think Buchanan's on to us. He knew about Mason. Offered money to have Soren returned to him. He was in a hurry about that, too, and I don't think it's the father in him that's missing his son." He continued to scratch his chin, eyes flicking across the shaded property. "Buchanan won't want to miss a chat with Mason. And I'm willing to bet he has a few things to say to the kid. He'll—"

Two men stepped around the side of the house and sauntered down the driveway. They wore similar expressions of arrogance and suits expensive enough to blend into The Smile's business surroundings, not to mention roomy enough to conceal weapons.

Ben reached for his gun on the seat next to him and flicked off the safety.

"Easy. Let's not have a shoot-out on a public street," Stoney said and straightened. "My job's circling the drain as it is."

Buchanan's men came to stand just outside the gate. The taller guy slowly flicked open his suit jacket, revealing a shoulder holster. He shoved his hands deep inside his pockets and struck a casual pose. The message was clear. He was as reluctant to disturb the calm afternoon as Stoney, but perfectly capable and willing to do so if pushed. His gaze swept over Ben and settled on Stoney. "You're the cop?"

"Yes."

"Your friend"—he nodded at Ben—"has been loitering."

"He'll be on his way just as soon as my brother comes

out."

"Yeah, about that. Mr. Buchanan asked us to deliver a message."

Ben tensed.

Stoney casually leaned back against the car, blocking most of the driver side window, shielding Ben. Ben silently cursed the Ward need to protect and peered around Stoney's considerable bulk. He saw the shorter of the two goons smirking.

"He'll be out shortly. Just as soon as Mr. Buchanan has a chance to talk to him in person. There's no need to wait. Mr. Buchanan will see to it that he's brought home."

Ben snorted. Fat chance.

"I think we'll wait," Stoney said.

"Suit yourself."

Ben didn't relax his grip on the Smith & Wesson until he saw Buchanan's men round the villa again. "What was that all about?"

Stoney leaned back into the open window. "Slick bastard's trying to avoid a kidnapping charge. Any luck getting in touch with Kaoru yet?"

Ben shook his head. Mason had tried a few times, never getting past his friend's voicemail. When he'd finally called the office, he'd been informed that Kaoru was expected to be at the courthouse all day (where neither service weapons nor cell phones were allowed). "Now what?"

"Now we wait."

19

Hoping to alleviate his dizziness, Mason stretched out on the futon, which immediately protested his weight with an ominous creak. He shot Soren a quick glance to see if the noise had made it past the redhead's brooding, but Soren kept prowling their prison, oblivious. His restless energy fueled by drugs and alcohol.

Mason groaned and scrubbed a hand over his face. Soren wasn't the only frustrated one. He thought of the kisses they'd shared and felt his pulse quicken. On impulse, he swung his legs over the edge of the creaking futon and pushed himself to his feet, ignoring the pounding headache and roiling nausea, determined to corner the redhead.

But the lock tumbled and clicked.

Mason swore.

Soren froze.

The Smile's men had shown up some time ago. First they'd knocked. Then they'd laughed about their clever humor—the room's occupants hardly able to refuse entry, although Mason could have bolted the heavy door from the inside. One of the over-paid, under-qualified bodyguards had told him that Mr. Buchanan wanted a word with Mason in the late afternoon. Thus, Mason was to remain with Soren and wait.

He could only guess that his wait was over now.

Sure enough, two of The Smile's men swept into the room. The taller and bulkier of the two roughly seized Mason by the arm, a mistake Mason made him regret an instant later when he flattened the guy's face against the tiled floor.

"I don't think so," Mason ground out. He increased the pressure of his left knee, keeping the man pinned to the floor. He applied just enough pressure to a locked right wrist and elbow to keep the guy's arm from breaking. He turned cold eyes on the second character who'd wisely remained by the door meeting Mason's hard stare with a smirk, obviously reveling in his co-worker's bad luck.

"Mr. Buchanan wants to talk to you," the guy said and jerked his chin in the direction of the kitchen.

Mason didn't move. He had to give the rest of his body time to catch up with his reflexes. He silently thanked his lucky stars that the man squirming under his knee didn't know enough to break his hold and fight back. He glanced up at Soren who looked at him with bright eyes and an inscrutable expression.

"Not him. He stays," the man at the door said curtly.

Mason hesitated.

"Let's go. Mr. Buchanan's not waiting all day."

"Go," Soren urged quietly.

"I'd listen to him if I were you." Mason flicked his eyes in the direction of the speaker, a third guy filing into the small room. Unlike the other two, he didn't wear a suit jacket, exposing a handgun slung under his left arm. He nodded at his man still pinned under Mason's knee. "Please don't break him. I still need him. Good muscle is hard to find these days." He arched his brows over challenging dark eyes, and Mason got the message. With great reluctance, he eased off the man he'd felled.

The latecomer nodded at his fallen comrade, who scrambled to his feet, glaring and rubbing his sore shoulder. "Son of a bitch," he spat. He straightened to his full height, likely used to towering over people, then had to look up to meet Mason's glacial stare. "Fuck," he added to a string of grumbled four-letter words, still rubbing his shoulder.

Sending his own message, Mason turned away from Buchanan's men. He met Soren's searching gaze with a smile, but the answering twitch of Soren's lips told him that the redhead didn't put much stock in their continued friendship. Soren's face seemed almost translucent, his freckles in stark relief to the paleness of his skin. Mason's hormones surged.

"Trust me," he said. "I will be back for you." He swallowed the awareness that rose with his promise and turned abruptly to stride past the snickering bodyguards and out of the room. He watched with expressionless eyes as the storm door was locked again, leaving Soren by himself. He didn't protest the rough patting down he received or the manhandling down a hallway into an airy study.

He would have expected The Smile to be a connoisseur of ridiculously expensive, finger-thick cigars, but there wasn't a trace of smoke in the air. On the contrary, the humid afternoon air that lazily drifted in through the open window louvers carried the fragrance of plumeria.

"Mr. Ward, please, have a seat." James gestured toward the overstuffed chairs in front of his desk. He lounged in his chair with the same casualness Mason had affected just moments before. This was his home, his office, his turf.

He was impeccably dressed in a gray suit—his silk tie was not loosened. Mason immediately saw why Soren did not think he was sorely in need of a haircut. His father's white hair was unfashionably long for a man his age, but it suited him. Much like the aura of power and authority that surrounded James, his mane was just another sign of his virility.

"Mr. Ward—"

"Mr. Buchanan."

James's pale blue eyes narrowed, evidently not used to being interrupted. "I am a busy man, so allow me to get right to the point. Soren is a troubled boy. He has, how shall I put this, problems with alcohol and drugs. Sometimes he—"

"Falls down?"

"Excuse me?"

Mason sat. Mirroring James's guarded casualness, he leaned back and crossed one leg over the other. "You are an intelligent man, Mr. Buchanan, so I won't insult you by playing games. Soren was given into my care after he seemed to have had an unfortunate run-in with some fists." He'd also been drunk and most likely on some form of chemical escape, but Mason didn't see the need to mention that. He met James's pale glare with expressionless eyes as he said, "He mentioned he embarrassed you."

James's nostrils flared.

"After a week with Soren, I can understand wanting to lay hands on him," Mason said. In more ways than one, his brain piped up. He squelched those thoughts ruthlessly. "But I am a grown man, Mr. Buchanan, and I can control my impulses." The memories of their kisses and the feel of Soren's cock in his fist flashed through Mason's mind. He shifted, uncrossed his legs, and planted both feet firmly on the thick carpet.

James had commendable control over his features and his voice, but he could not suppress the hard glint of anger in his blue eyes. "I thank you for his safety, Mr. Ward. I understand he returned voluntarily. Nevertheless, I offered to pay for his return." He opened a leather-bound folder in front of him, extracted a check made out to Mason and slid it across the table. "I am a man of my word."

Mason took the check and a lazy look at the six-figure number scrawled on it. He whistled.

"I would appreciate it if you forgot about Soren. My son"—James stressed the family connection—"is no longer your concern."

Mason looked down at the check in his hands. There was enough there to pay off the Sprite's mortgage twice over and take care of her annual maintenance for some time to come. James Buchanan had to be seriously desperate. He already had his son back. There was no need for him to offer this kind of money. A wave of disgust rose in Mason at the thought of accepting the man's bribe, but he was fairly certain that James hadn't once considered Mason not accepting his offer. Still, Mason felt very little satisfaction when he placed the check back on the table, pushing it away from him.

"You are making a mistake."

"I don't think so."

"Very well then. I do not see any need to prolong this conversation." James rose and snapped his fingers. Immediately one of his bodyguards appeared in the doorway. "Escort Mr. Ward off my property. Make sure he meets up with his brother and his friend who are parked outside."

Mason got to his feet and shook off the hand that fell on his shoulder. "I'm not leaving without Soren."

"Mr. Ward." James pulled his fleshy lips into his trademark smile. His teeth gleamed, freshly bleached. "Mason. Soren stays. His mother has requested his presence, and I am inclined to grant her wish."

Mason didn't budge.

"Take the money or leave it. I do not care. But you do not want to test the limits of my patience. I would not recommend it."

Marshalling a casual air again, James sank back down onto his chair. He crossed his legs and folded his arms.

"Once my men have seen you safely outside, I intend to have a talk with my son. After all he has made you believe about me, do you really think it is wise to rouse my temper, Mr. Ward?"

Mason turned to see his three-man escort. Their eager expressions clearly told him they'd relish the chance to manhandle him out of the house and down the driveway. Mason turned back to face James and met The Smile's icy glare with a challenge in his own eyes. "I'll be back for him."

20

James seethed. He paced his office with angry strides. He was sick of being embarrassed and humiliated by his own flesh and blood. Soren was deliberately and maliciously ruining everything James had worked for.

James came to an abrupt stop in front of his massive desk. Forty years of his life down the drain because of his own son. He was not going to let that happen. But what riled his temper more than the betrayal was his failure as a father. How could he have failed so spectacularly with Soren?

The doors to the study burst open, followed by Soren stumbling inside, ahead of a few of The Smile's men.

"You," James snarled as he balled up his fists. "You ungrateful little bastard!"

James raised his right hand, but didn't unclench his fist as he delivered a backhand to his son. Soren tumbled into the desk, sending papers and an Italian glass weight flying. Soren's right leg gave out, and he went down hard on one knee.

James struggled to control his temper. He clenched his teeth, and the muscles in his jaw jumped. He had promised Caren that he would not do anything rash, and he was not about to break his word. Unlike his son, he knew the meaning of integrity. What he was about to do was not impulsive; he had thought it through. He would rein in Soren with a demonstration, show him what life would really be like if he was half as mean as his son made him out to be. Soren was lucky that James was not like his own father. The man had been a vicious and unpredictable disciplinarian, a drunk who beat his wife and children with little provocation.

James stepped behind his desk, surveying the mess Soren's flailing had produced. One of the papers strewn across the floor had to be the check the stubborn Ward declined. The irony of the moment was not lost on James. Soren was about to receive exactly what he had whined to the Ward brothers about—as if beatings were a regular occurrence.

Looking directly into Soren's bright eyes James said, "I give you a home and a job. I pay your bills. I indulge your little hobby. And what do I get in return?"

James unbuttoned his suit jacket, shrugged out of it and tossed it over his chair. He watched Soren's eyes follow the path of the jacket, before they snapped back, and his lips curled in disgust. Strung out on drugs and booze, no doubt, which explained his state of undress, but not the uncharacteristic silence.

"You know how I hate to be disappointed. And you have been nothing but a disappointment lately."

Soren brushed the back of his hand across his bleeding mouth and shook his head. He shrugged off the hands that held him and steadied himself on the edge of the desk. His glare carried no heat.

"You went to the FBI. You betrayed me. Your family. Our name. Did you think I would not know? You think I do not know what goes on in my house? In my town?" James thought of the FBI snooping around, about the Ward brothers and their questions, their suspicions and accusations. Soren's actions had invited outsiders in and that was inexcusable. "I have tried. God knows, I have tried. But you—" He stepped out from behind his desk, gesturing wildly, not finding the right words to express his frustration.

"Yeah, right," Soren sneered. "So sorry about fucking up your life."

James snapped. He yanked his belt free and, for a moment, remembered his own father doing the very same thing to him. And the acute embarrassment the whipping had cost him. Yes, it would be a fitting punishment. And unlike his earlier arguments with Soren, always private and behind closed doors, he intended this one to be a public humiliation; he had no intention of dismissing his men.

His pent-up anger and frustration made him wield the belt without restraint or accuracy. He meant to hurt, period, not caring where the leather bit into Soren's skin or if the belt buckle tore a bloody gash across an upraised arm. He did not stop raining down lashes when Soren dropped to the floor in an unresisting heap, nor did he stop when the belt was slick with his sweat and Soren's blood.

By the time his rage abated, the belt lay forgotten on the floor and his men had withdrawn to a corner of the room. Blood flecked his shirt sleeves, and sweat pearled on his upper lip. Unhappy with his loss of control, James stalked over to his bar. He poured bottled water over ice then gulped down the cool liquid and waved away his men. Damn the boy for driving him to this.

Soren was on the floor, curled on his side. His eyes were closed, his breathing labored, his bare chest smeared with blood. James cursed the fair complexion he had so enjoyed on Caren. Soren would be black and blue within hours.

He would not be able to ship the boy off to his mother for at least another ten days. Even then, James was not at all happy with the idea of Soren spending time with Caren and her parents. They gave him ideas James did not appreciate.

"You made a mistake," Soren croaked. "I didn't turn on you."

His temper spent, James did not bother turning. He poured himself another glass of water.

"I didn't betray your precious name," Soren insisted. "They asked," he said. "They—"

"Oh, so they tricked you? The FBI made you tell them? Please do not insult me with your lies and stories." James turned. He watched his son struggle to his feet, having trouble with his right leg. James did not recall having gone near Soren's legs. Bruises were one thing, an injury was quite another. As it was, he would have to make sure Soren stayed confined to the house until the evidence of his beating faded.

"I told you I have eyes and ears all over this island. Do you really think I do not know what is going on here? You were seen walking into their offices, Soren. Are you going to tell me you met that Mason character in one of your clubs? Do not insult me with your lies and stories."

Soren shook his head. "Yeah, I talked to the feds. But not about you," he spat, still defiant. "This little lecture of yours." He snorted. "You wasted your time. I didn't betray you. I ... Jolina—"

James slid into his chair. "You turned her in?"

Soren nodded.

James laughed. Oh, this was interesting. "You dumb shit. If you think you hurt now, just wait until they are done with you."

21

"What the hell?" Mason's eyes swung from his refrigerator door to his brother on the Sprite's side deck just outside the galley door, cell phone pressed to his ear. "Someone shot my fridge." He pulled the door open to a soggy mess. A quick check assured him that the back of his refrigerator was still intact. By the looks of the mess, the jug of milk had taken the brunt of the assault.

"Relax." Stoney shouldered his way past Mason. "He wasn't aiming for it."

Mason sighed and reached for the sponge he kept by the sink, then thought better of it and closed the refrigerator with uncharacteristic indifference. He'd clean it later. Right now he had more important things to do. If he wanted to tell Soren in person that he didn't appreciate holes in his appliances, they'd have to figure out a way to get the redhead out of his father's house first.

Stoney had called in a few favors and one of his friends from patrol was already on his way to the Buchanan residence to follow up on the missing persons report filed by Soren's mother. Mason didn't think for a minute that a cop showing up at his doorstep would do much to intimidate The Smile, but at the very least it ought to have James think twice before doing anything careless.

They needed Kaoru, but the fed was still incommunicado.

"So?" Stoney drawled.

"Drop it, Stone."

"We were waiting out there all afternoon, while you and Soren...you know, we're curious."

Ben, shaking raindrops from his hair, trailed Stoney inside and groaned. "Not me. No, siree." He closed the heavy door to the side deck. "Starting to get wet out there."

The perky announcer on the car radio had changed her tune from tropical storm to possible typhoon. Miserable weather either way, but it suited Mason's bad mood. He stalked into his office where his phone lay ringing on his desk, Kaoru's number on the display. He snatched it up and dropped into the chair behind his desk.

"Yes?"

"Tell me you've got the kid," Kaoru said.

"I've got The Smile trying to bribe and threaten me. I've got my ass kicked off his property, and one hell of a headache."

"No kid, I take it."

"No," Mason ground out between clenched teeth. "I nearly had my skull cracked. There is a gaping hole in my fridge, and there was a dead woman in my living room." The coroner had taken the corpse, but left the mess. Mason groaned. He'd have to clean that, too. "I would have appreciated you telling me from the beginning what the hell was going on here. I might not have walked in on Soren and his terrorist girlfriend totally clueless."

Mason delivered a condensed first-hand account that covered the events of the last seventeen hours, filling the holes in his recollection with the information Soren, Stoney and Ben had provided.

Kaoru said, "There's nothing much for me to go on here. If this was an adult kidnapping, I could swing some sort of official interest after seventy-two hours. But the kid went home voluntarily. And Buchanan didn't lock you in that closet. You got the kid on record about recognizing his father's muscle?"

"No."

"Of course not."

"What the hell is that supposed to mean?"

"Whoa. Relax."

Mason scrubbed a hand over his face before reaching up to massage away the pounding behind his right temple. "What about the girlfriend?"

"Man, I've been on the phone with our attaché in the Philippines all week. I guess her name has come up in connection with some local crimes, but if she did kill an American, she picked one who wouldn't be missed. Right now I don't even have enough to pick her up and send her home."

"We need to get into that house, Kaoru. I want Soren out of there. Official or not." Mason scooted back to pull open the bottom drawer of his desk. A gun safe was bolted down inside. He thumbed in the push-button combination and opened the lid to his back-up Beretta and the extra magazines he kept.

"I might have something," Stoney said from the doorway. He had his cell phone in his hand. "They just identified the dead woman. Carmen Quinata. Six priors, two outstanding misdemeanor warrants, and one conviction for terroristic threatening and kidnapping."

"How does that help us?"

"What helps us are her known associates," Stoney continued undeterred. "One Carl Cruz, in particular. Her cousin. And get this, he happens to be employed by James Buchanan."

Kaoru's curse traveled over the phone line with such clarity that even Stoney heard him. He took the phone from his brother's grasp. "Yo, I've got a black-and-white on the way. According to his mother, Cruz is still at work. We're in luck, he's on the late shift. It's not much, but it ought to get the guys past the front door for a little chat. And Buchanan strikes me as just arrogant enough to let them look around some."

Mason didn't hear what his friend had to say to Stoney, but he could tell by his brother's face that Kaoru's words fell short of Stoney's expectations.

"Fine," Stoney grumbled, before he gave back the phone and stalked off.

"What did you tell him?"

"I told him to stay put. Actually, I'd rather you guys meet me at my office. Where are you right now?"

"On the Sprite."

"Listen, I'll make a few calls, and I'll swing by the Buchanan place. It's not official, but since Soren came to see me, and I'm almost certain his father knows that, I can blame curiosity. Speaking of which—"Kaoru's tone betrayed his grin—"just how much money did he offer?"

Mason's lips twitched, but he remained quiet.

Kaoru sighed. "I take it he pays better for returning his son than I do for keeping him."

"And it would have been tax-free, too."

22

From the other side of the bathroom door Carl Cruz sounded annoyed. "Hurry on up in there." He pounded on the door once more, adding a string of curses to his urging.

"Screw you," Soren hissed. He didn't move from his precarious sitting position on the rim of his bathtub. It wasn't sitting as much as a delicate leaning of sorts. He'd tried standing, but his right hip—bruised to the bone—didn't tolerate the weight very well. Sitting wasn't much better—it hurt like hell—but at least the sour churning in his stomach subsided somewhat.

He couldn't be sure, but he figured he was living the worst day of his life. And, yes, that included begging Mason to fuck him. What the hell had he been thinking? He groaned and rested his head against the cool tile of the bathroom wall.

He could blame the drugs and alcohol all he wanted. The truth was he'd been curious well before he'd met Mason, and now his appetite had been whetted. He'd gotten a taste of male hands on him, and he'd liked it. He didn't think he was supposed to like it. Something about sin and brimstone. As if he had to worry about offending a higher power. His father would go ballistic when he found out that one of his trophy sons considered batting for the other team. A wry smile pulled on Soren's split lip. He was pretty sure his father didn't think he could sink any lower, be any less of a disappointment or any more difficult. Yeah, there'd be hell to pay, no doubt.

"Hurry on up in there. What's taking so long?"

"Fuck off."

"You wish."

Soren shifted, which garnered him a sharp pain across his pelvis. He caught his grimace in the mirror and suppressed another groan. He hadn't looked this bad in a long time. Bruises were starting to bloom across his shoulders and ribs. Angry, red welts covered his chest and arms—and his back as well. The right side of his face was red and swollen from brow bone to jaw, his right eyelid puffy with the promise of a truly spectacular shiner. There were still fading bruises on his face from the last time he'd been on the receiving end of his father's anger. Hell, it had only been a week since he'd climbed out his bedroom window to call Kaoru with enough information to barter for protection.

He'd never had youthful aspirations to become a spy or secret agent. The name Soren Buchanan didn't sound nearly as macho as James Bond, and for all his love of alcohol, he couldn't stand martinis. Spying really wasn't his thing. But he'd willingly climbed into bed with Jolina, because that's where she shared her secrets. Okay, and he'd been curious about the drugs. He sighed. He'd been curious about sex with Mason, too. Curiosity sucked.

This whole Mason thing, though, it was different. It felt

different. That was no adolescent crush, no hormonal infatuation, hell, no curiosity, he felt. He knew that Mason hadn't just walked out on him. His trust in that knowledge, his total conviction that Mason would be back for him, was a clue about as subtle as his near-panic attack at the thought of losing Mason to a bullet.

Soren flashed his mirror image a shaky smile.

Mason was the first person to see past his obvious flaws and his attitude. He'd seen potential where no one else had. He'd been quite vocal about that. He'd certainly not bought into any of the many excuses Soren had at the ready.

Soren might have complained and bitched about it, but the truth was he'd bought into his father's agenda. He'd seen no other choice than to fall in line and do as was expected of him. His only option had been to delay the inevitable as long as possible. Damn, he'd been brainwashed!

"Your girlfriend's here," Carl Cruz announced gleefully outside the bathroom door. "Hurry on up in there."

Soren caught himself staring into his own eyes. He took a deep breath that sounded (and felt) suspiciously like a sob. Damn.

This was it; the chance to decide the rest of his life. He could walk out of his bathroom a victim or stand up for himself and become the man Mason thought he could be. Maybe, if he made an effort to become that man, there was a future for him out there. With Mason. He was intensely aware of the man's absence.

"You can't hide in there forever. Get your ass out here or I'm coming in there to get you."

"Bite me," Soren shot back. He heaved himself to his feet and crossed the tiny distance to the sink.

His worst day ever hadn't ended yet. His father had negotiated some sort of deal with the Miciano family that involved handing over his son for a private chat—his father's euphemism for "take you away and kick the shit out of you for being stupid enough to talk to the FBI about Jolina, her cousins and their warped world view."

He grabbed a wash cloth and began to clean the blood off

his chest, when a sudden idea struck him.

"I'm coming in. One. Two—"

Soren unlocked the door and yanked it open before Cruz could do any damage to it. He stepped past the hired muscle into his adjoining bedroom. The bathroom door fell closed behind him.

"Thought you'd gotten lost in there," Cruz grumbled.

Soren didn't bother with a reply. He limped to the armchair next to his bed and rifled through the haphazardly folded mountain of clothes, searching for a T-shirt.

"You're a slob," Cruz spat derisively.

Soren shrugged. At least he wasn't an asshole. But he was careful not to voice his thoughts, very conscious of the man carrying a gun and a grudge.

It didn't help that Cruz was right.

His bed was a rumpled mess—excusable, since he'd left it rather abruptly—but the rest of his room didn't fare much better. An empty champagne bottle kept two not-so-empty coffee mugs and a crumpled soda can company on the nightstand. A surfboard, precariously angled and wedged into a corner, doubled as a coat rack. The armchair next to his bed was home to more clothes than the closet whose gaping doors were prevented from closing by an assortment of shoes spilling out of it. His stereo equipment was drowning beneath a sea of CDs and a volleyball. Old newspaper sections, mail, receipts, notes and other loose-leafed paperwork were stacked on top of the TV and strewn across the desk. Soren was fairly sure that some of those papers were college homework he'd never turned in. Maybe he'd clean up after all this was over. No, he had no intention of returning. Ever. Not even to pack. He'd have Mason stop by for his passports.

The thought of Mason stepping into his room had him grinning—the man would be overcome by his freakish cleaning and straightening impulses for sure—but the view from the balustrade down the sweeping stairs made Soren break out in a cold sweat a moment later.

Sure enough, Cruz took great pleasure in prodding Soren

whenever his hip and leg threatened to give out. By the time they reached his father's office, Soren was glad for Cruz's hands on him. He did his best to keep up mock resistance, lest his father's muscle realize he actually needed the help staying on his feet.

Flanked by Cruz and another of his father's cronies who'd materialized suddenly, he got his first look at Eleoterio and Timoteo Miciano. Jolina's cousins didn't look like dangerous, murderous rebels. But then—Soren's eyes swung to Jolina—neither did the petite brunette in the clingy silk top and the flirty little skirt. She saw him looking and locked gazes with him for a moment. No, she hadn't forgotten about her promise to kill him herself either.

He had hoped her cousins would be more imposing. Like a darker, more dangerous version of Mason. Tall, muscular and fairly screaming "don't fuck with me or I'll snap your scrawny neck with one hand." Even knowing what they were capable of, it was difficult to be intimidated by two beach boys in floral shirts and baggy shorts after he'd spent a week staring down hulking Mason. Still, even lacking the height and bulk it took to appear as much of a physical threat, they were dangerous and probably used to being underestimated.

Soren had no plans to underestimate Eleoterio and Timoteo Miciano. Despite James's deal, which required that his son still be alive at the end of the night, Soren figured his chances of making it until dawn would improve greatly if he didn't act like the asshole they thought he was. Ironically, standing up for himself and becoming his own man would have to start with him acting meek and repentant. Cowering would probably also help. He probably could do submissive and docile if he had to.

"Let's go," Timoteo snapped.

The second he said it Soren's eyes were on him. Despite the fierce pain throbbing across his hip, Soren stood up straighter, which only aggravated the hurt that was his back and generally the rest of him. But he met Timoteo's dark eyes with an unflinching look of his own. The sentiment was clear. Fuck off. Too late Soren remembered that he'd wanted to go for meek and submissive, but it just wasn't in him to cower. Timoteo smiled, and the hairs along Soren's arms rose.

"Let's go," Jolina's cousin repeated, impatience coloring his voice.

James gestured and his men moved aside. Immediately, Jolina stepped up to Soren and took him by the elbow, steering him toward the door. "Just do what they say," she whispered. "They just want to talk," she added. The "unless it was you who betrayed me" remained unsaid.

"You still got that gun in your purse?" Soren asked from between clenched teeth. Each step was a red-hot, electric jolt of agony across his hip and pelvis. In a way, he welcomed the pain. It kept him focused. This was still it; his chance to change the direction of his life (if he survived the night, that was). Either way, he wouldn't return, the outcome of his talk with the cousins notwithstanding. He had no real idea if a life away from his father's influence was possible, but he'd try his damnedest to get out from under the man's thumb, starting right now.

"The gun? Yes," Jolina said.

"Shoot me now and be done with it?"

"You wish," Timoteo interjected, coming between his cousin and Soren. "First, there'll be screaming, then there'll be shooting."

23

Despite evening rush hour being over and the fact that Stoney completely ignored the posted 35-mph speed limit, it took the brothers more than twice the time it should have to reach Mongmong. Torrential rain reduced visibility to zero. Gusting winds tried pushing Stoney's Jeep into every flooded pothole on Marine Drive, making the older twin curse and swerve with great abandon, which, in turn, aggravated the killer headache pounding inside Mason's skull.

"Nasty out there," Stoney said when he finally pulled to a stop in front of the First Hawaiian Bank building. "You okay? You're a bit green around the gills."

Mason gave his brother a peeved glare.

"You have a concussion."

Mason made a conscious effort to relax his jaw and unclench his balled fists. He hadn't felt this bad in a long time, but the pain that sliced through his brain was only partially due to the toaster oven he'd dented with his skull. Guilt, regret and the knowledge that he'd failed added their strength to the axe hacking away at him behind his eyes.

"You should be lying in bed, taking it easy."

"I'm fine." Mason ground his teeth at his brother's concern. He'd go to sleep in his darkened bedroom just as soon as he knew Soren was okay. He even intended to swallow a handful of the over-the-counter painkillers Stoney had brought him with breakfast. The rest he'd flush so as not to tempt Soren. Mason cringed when that thought caught up with him. Chances were the redhead would have no reason to come back aboard the Sprite. Disappointment tore through Mason at the realization. He wanted Soren to come back to him.

"Christ." He scrubbed a hand down his face and groaned. "I'm screwed."

Stoney opened his mouth to share whatever opinion he had on the matter, but Mason was quicker. "Don't say it. Don't even think it. Let's just go up there and talk to Kaoru."

Thankfully, Stoney, heeding only part of his brother's advice, limited his response to a cocky grin. They dashed through the rain toward the First Hawaiian Bank building that housed the FBI office suite, dodging airborne palm fronds whipped about by driving winds.

Kaoru frowned at them when they plopped into the chairs in front of his desk. His glance swept past their shoulders to the door. "Where's Ben?"

"On his way home." Mason hadn't seen a need for his friend to continue to chauffeur him around when Ben could be with his family, catching up on sleep. Plus, someone had to show up at the office in the morning, and Mason didn't think that was going to be him.

"I would have liked to talk to him," Kaoru grumbled.

Stoney rolled his eyes at that. "So call him."

Mason, who knew Kaoru better than his brother, had the

sinking feeling that the agent's bad mood had something to do with his recent visit to the Buchanan house. "What's up?"

Kaoru nodded in Stoney's direction. "You were right. Buchanan's an arrogant son of a bitch. He had the nerve to ask if my showing up had anything to do with the rumors Soren had heard about his girlfriend. Apparently, concerned father that he is, James had sensed some tension between his son and the girlfriend when she came to pick him up."

Mason ground his teeth. If this kept up, he'd have to get dental work. "Soren wasn't there?"

"No. But we must have just missed him, because they didn't have time to clean up after him yet." Kaoru broke into a wide, humorless grin. "I'm willing to bet heads are rolling and Buchanan's spilling blood over this right now." He unfolded his cell phone and scrolled through the menu options before finding the picture he'd taken inside Soren's bathroom. He handed the opened phone over to Mason. "I'm guessing that's a clue."

Curious, Stoney leaned over to have a look at the small display. "Is that blood?"

"Yes. The cops found the message in the kid's bathroom while I was still talking to Buchanan."

It was a bloody square smeared on a mirror. Inside the square, two diagonals crossed from opposite corners, creating an X.

"X marks the spot?" Kaoru asked.

"I'll be damned," mumbled Mason.

"Huh?"

"That's the letter V."

"I know I only went to public school, but that doesn't look like a V to me."

Mason shook his head. "No. The symbol. It's a representation of a signal flag. The Victor flag. I'll be damned."

"I don't get it."

"He's got the most mule-headed brain, I swear. He can't navigate to save his life, but he takes one look at my signal flag chart and remembers."

"Told you it was a clue." But Kaoru still didn't get it. "So what the hell does it mean?"

"Require assistance."

"He knew something was up."

Mason nodded. Dread over the situation still churned his stomach. He had more questions than answers—like where the hell had the blood come from?—and not nearly enough information to go by. Even Kaoru's detailed recall of his conversation with The Smile and exploration of the house did little to alleviate his fear that Soren's situation had gone from bad to worse.

"Where does all that leave us?" he asked after a long moment of silence that had given the men a chance to digest what had and hadn't been said.

"Screwed," Stoney said.

Kaoru shrugged.

"Shit." Mason pushed to his feet. He stepped out of Kaoru's office and into the cubicle area most of the other agents shared. Desk lamps were on here and there, but he didn't see anyone else around. He couldn't remember the last time he'd been here during regular office hours. Long, angry strides carried him to the men's room off the lobby. He took one look at his reflection in the mirror and cursed. There were dark circles under his bruised eyes and lines around his mouth that hadn't been there the last time he'd seen himself. Christ, he'd aged ten years since then.

Stoney waited for him in the lobby.

"Just got a call. The skipper of the charter yacht that followed Ben just stumbled into an ER."

Mason nodded. He was certain this whole mess could have been avoided if he hadn't met up with Ben again after they'd spotted the charter yacht the first time. He called himself all kinds of stupid for not continuing on in the opposite direction.

"Unlike you, he might have gotten a look at Cruz before they beat him senseless," Stoney continued.

Mason sneered. "Buchanan offered me a small fortune to walk away. He's going to buy this guy his own fleet to forget who attacked him."

"Probably." Stoney pushed away from the wall he was leaning against and stabbed the elevator's down button. "So let's go talk to him before amnesia sets in. I don't care if he drops the charges later. Right now, with any luck, he can give us what we need to put the screws to Cruz."

"What about Kaoru?"

Stoney shrugged.

Mason arched his brows.

Stoney crossed his arms over his muscular chest and stared hard at the lit elevator button. "They encouraged him, you know?"

"They? Encouraged who? Kaoru? What?"

Stoney passed a droll look to his twin. "Kaoru and Buchanan. They. Encouraged Soren." He glanced back over his shoulder at the federal office suite. "Kaoru should have put a wire on Soren, given him some guidance, taken him seriously. He just sent Soren right back in there without any backup. And Buchanan? Don't get me started on that asshole. The man basically prostituted his son to keep his business relationship with Miciano intact. Fuck, I'd drink, too."

Mason hiked a brow at his brother. "You like Soren."

"He's got spunk," Stoney said.

"He's trouble."

The older Ward nodded.

"I can't just walk away, Stone."

"I know."

Mason rolled his eyes. He glowered at his twin, then admitted, "We kissed."

"I figured."

Mason snorted. "No, you figured we had sex."

Stoney's face broke into a broad grin. "He'd keep you on your toes. He'd drive you nuts, and you'd love it."

"He would, wouldn't he?" Mason sighed and answered his brother's foolish grin with one of his own. "Damn, I've got the hots for that kid."

Stoney's laughter filled the small elevator car as the doors slid open. "You're in way over your head, bro."

24

Jolina, her cousins and Soren arrived at their destination after a bone-jarring ride that had to have been Eleoterio purposely aiming the van at every single pothole. Soren was almost sure of it. How could the guy have missed seeing the gaping holes in the road?

Bruised and aching, Soren climbed from the van just as the flood gates in the sky opened. Flanked by Jolina and Timoteo, he stood in the driveway of a nondescript single-family home—the Guamanian euphemism for "small concrete bunker"—with a tiny lawn parched brown after a hot summer, getting drenched. He pointed at the house and asked, "What's this?"

"A house," Eleoterio hissed before hurrying inside.

Soren rolled his eyes. "What? No dark lair? I was thinking abandoned airstrip, rusty junkyard. You know—"

"Shut up, Soren." Jolina hissed at his side, yanking at his arm. Wet silk clung to her breasts. "You watch too much television."

Soren swallowed a comment—he couldn't remember the last time he'd watched TV—and swiped wet hair out of his face. Meek and repentant, he told himself. As long as he remembered to keep any challenging to a minimum, he would somehow get out of this.

He had the distinct feeling that Jolina and her cousins didn't think he was capable of more than mouthing off and cowering. Despite his newfound resolve to stand up for himself—or as Mason had put it, to be on his own side—he saw no problem in keeping up old appearances for a while longer.

"Move it," Timoteo snapped. He lifted his brightly colored shirt and let Soren have a look at the butt of a gun sticking out of the waistband of his shorts. Soren noticed the placement and angle of the muzzle over the guy's crotch and cringed. Wasn't he afraid he'd accidentally shoot his balls off? Then again, the guy was a hardened criminal—Soren snickered—he probably had balls of steel and bullets bounced right off.

Soren sighed. If he wanted to get out of this unscathed he needed to pay attention, not crack jokes. Where the hell were they anyway? He'd been so busy on the ride over trying not to pass out that he hadn't paid attention to their route. "So who lives here?"

Timoteo herded him toward the stairs just inside a tiny foyer as he said, "No one."

Soren didn't believe him. He had to crane his neck to catch a glimpse of the living room, but what he saw—a comfortable couch in front of an Asian-inspired entertainment center, framed family photographs on cheerfully yellow walls—was tastefully decorated and obviously lived in.

Timoteo noticed Soren looking around and smirked. "Forget it. They won't find you here. It's just a house. We appropriated it." With practiced ease, Timoteo extracted his gun and pointed up the stairs. "Move it."

Soren bit back a nasty reply and started climbing the stairs. He eyed the family pictures on the wall. None of them looked remotely familiar. None of them looked Filipino. If this was really just some random house, no one was going to come barging in to rescue him. He was on his own.

Timoteo prodded him down a hallway, past closed doors and framed, crayoned kid art. At the gaping door to a small guest bathroom, Soren balked.

"Bathrooms," Timoteo mused, waving his gun. "Tile. So easy to clean. Blood washes right off."

Soren thought of his bathroom and made a face. "I'll take your word for it," he mumbled.

When Soren made no move to enter the bathroom, Timoteo gave him a shove, then gleefully enjoyed the show as Soren tried to regain his balance without putting too much weight on his right leg.

Timoteo toed the drain set in the floor. "You unscrew this and wash everything right down there. The people who live here, they'll come back and won't ever know." He pulled a pair of handcuffs out of his pocket and dangled them in front of Soren. "Put these on."

It was like walking into a brick wall. Soren took a step forward to reach the cuffs and walked straight into Timoteo's curled fist, driven into Soren's stomach. He dropped into an uppercut that snapped his head back and left him on the floor, staring at the bathroom ceiling and gasping for air. Blood filled his mouth. Soren rolled to his side and coughed the blood on the drain.

Timoteo squatted down next to him. "When I'm done with you, you won't be so pretty anymore. Now, put these on."

Soren had no choice but to handcuff his left wrist to a towel bar that didn't budge when Timoteo gave it an experimental tug. Then the bathroom door was locked and for the second time that day Soren found himself in a dark room with nothing to do.

He thought he saw shapes, not that there was much to see

to begin with, a sink, a toilet, and a bathtub shrouded by a shower curtain. The room was just big enough to keep him from the door, handcuffed as he was.

He ran his right hand across the walls closest to him, looking for a light switch. He knocked a ceramic toothbrush holder off the edge of the sink and sent it clattering into the sink. He found a curling iron and eventually a night light. By its soft glow, he towel dried his hair, sat on the toilet—a cushioned seat, how luxurious—and thought about his blood staining the cream-colored tiles. He didn't care for the color combination. He wondered if his bloody drawing had been discovered yet and why the hell he hadn't just written Help.

Mason would understand his message, Soren thought. Both his messages; the one that said Help and the one that said Soren had actually paid attention while on board the Sprite.

Soren listened intently for noises from downstairs. He caught snatches of an argument whenever someone raised their voice—it was enough to tell him that the cousins were occupied with each other. But a moment later, he heard the front door slam, and his stomach sank. He had the uneasy feeling that Jolina had just turned her back on him, leaving her cousins to do with him as they pleased.

Soren ineffectually yanked on the handcuff around his wrist and the short chain tethering him to the towel bar. He wasn't going to slip the stainless steel off without damage to his wrist, but he had enough scrapes and bruises and no intention of willfully inflicting more.

With trepidation he transferred his attention to the towel bar. With any luck it wouldn't be the kind of bar set solidly into a concrete wall, but rather held in place by small screws drilled into sheetrock and plywood.

He yanked and pulled and started to sweat. He hissed when sweat ran down his arm and across the bloody gash his father's belt buckle had opened there. Then one of the anchors inside the wall gave way, slipped to the side, and the bar came loose. Soren almost toppled over the toilet. He jarred his hip and razor sharp pain sliced across his pelvis, into his thigh and up his spine. "Fuck," he gasped and slowly straightened. "Fucking A."

It was an odd time to remember, but Soren could clearly recall his horoscope in the newspaper Ben had brought with his provisions onboard the Sprite: The highly intelligent Scorpio excels at solving problems.

Soren grinned from the memory. He was stuck in a stranger's bathroom, handcuffs dangling from his left wrist, and the terrorists downstairs were out to get him. If that didn't qualify as a problem what did? Now he needed a solution. He opened the vanity door under the sink and found some toilet bowl cleaner with bleach. To the right of the toilet was a small trash can with cute cat faces and paw prints on its sides. He emptied the full bottle of toilet bowl cleaner into the trash can, then added some water.

Holding the trash can close, Soren walked up to the locked door and called out, "Hello? Any assholes out there? Excuse me!"

He waited for footsteps. None came, so he added, "There's something in here with me!"

Still nothing.

He took a deep breath then called out again, "I could use some help in here!"

Finally he heard muffled Filipino curses, then footsteps. He stepped back when he heard a key slide into the lock.

The bathroom door flew open and standing there was Eleoterio. Soren tossed the contents of the trash can into Eleoterio's face. The Filipino's hands flew up to protect his eyes, but the toilet bowl cleaner still splashed across unprotected skin and into his open mouth. Soren didn't give him a chance to do more than gurgle. He slammed the trash can against the side of Eleoterio's head. Eleoterio staggered into the door, bounced off it and into another swing of the trash can before sagging to the floor.

Soren froze. One heartbeat. Two heartbeats. The keys were on the floor where Eleoterio had dropped them. Soren quickly picked them up, then dragged Eleoterio's body farther into the bathroom. There was laughter coming from downstairs as Soren quietly closed the bathroom door and locked it. He took a moment to lean against the wall and take a shaky breath. His hip protested fiercely. The unrelenting pain across his pelvis and into this lower back had his stomach roiling with nausea.

Soren pocketed the bathroom key then pushed away from the wall and approached the stairs. He could see the front door from where he stood. He was one mad dash away from freedom, but silently creeping down the stairs would probably get him farther. He'd sneak out into the torrential rain and with any luck wouldn't be missed until he was at least one block away. His brilliant plan didn't include anything beyond running, which in his current state he wasn't exactly capable of doing.

He put his foot on the first step and heard Timoteo downstairs. The Filipino, cell phone pressed to his left ear, chatting in Tagalog, rounded the corner when Soren was half way down the stairs. They noticed each other at about the same time, but it was Soren who acted first. He lunged forward, bringing Timoteo down in a mad, flying tackle. Timoteo lost his phone and most of the air in his lungs when Soren slammed into him. The two of them fell onto the hardwood floor. Timoteo was on his feet first, hunched over, wheezing. Soren crouched low, then leapt up, smashing his shoulder into Timoteo's midsection. The Filipino was catapulted into the far wall.

Soren staggered to the front door.

Upstairs Eleoterio began pounding on the locked bathroom door.

Soren had his hand on the doorknob when Timoteo jumped on him. They crashed into the spindly table next to the door. It cracked under their combined weight, and they landed in a tangled heap on the hardwood floor again. Soren struggled, shoved, and kicked, but Timoteo clung to him, working his way up the long legs he held on to.

Desperate, Soren groped for something he could use among the debris surrounding him. He touched a solid object, brought it around and smashed it against Timoteo's head. The halogen lamp caught the Filipino across the side of the face. He slumped over Soren's legs. Soren put his considerable frustration behind it and swung the lamp twice more. Timoteo went slack.

"Screw you," Soren hissed. He dropped the lamp and rubbed his abused throat. "I like being pretty, thank you very much." He pushed the Filipino off him, climbed to his feet, opened the front door and dashed into pouring rain.

25

By the time Soren reached the end of the driveway he was soaked to the bone. At the end of the block he was panting through clenched teeth and severely pissed off. Sweat mingled with the rainwater running down his face.

He was in the middle of a residential neighborhood where every house was identical. Although it was night, Soren could see the dark shapes of rusted out cars and abandoned swings in the yards. There were no street lights and the sidewalk—which must have been poured before the Japanese overran Guam in 1941 and hadn't been repaired since—was hopelessly flooded.

Soren ran on, trying to forget about the pain racking his

body and the driving rain soaking his clothes. His worn tennis shoes sloshed with water. His jeans had become a leaden weight that not only dragged him down but threatened to slip off his hips. Smears of blood stained the front of his T-shirt, coloring the fabric an unbecoming pink.

The houses he passed were dark. No light spilled out of windows and into yards. It had to be close to midnight, which accounted for the lack of life, or so Soren hoped. He heard a car coming as he cut through a yard, and dashed behind some bushes, which was fraught with its own dangers: after the car had passed, Soren nearly stepped on a wild chicken. The bird squawked and ruffled its feathers as Soren quickly tried to get out of the way and fell over a rusted tricycle. He lay in the soggy grass, rain lashing him, until his heart rate returned to normal.

"Fucking shit," he mumbled as he stood, then continued his way through yards, ducking behind a bush every time he heard a car drive by.

Soren needed a phone. A pawn shop would do, too. Pawn shops usually came with burly guys with shotguns under the counter. Then again, he had yet to see one that was open at midnight. What he really needed was a freaking Circle K convenience store, open twenty-four hours, rain or shine.

What he found instead was Uncle Bob's Self Storage, 24/7 security, central air-conditioning, pest control, competitive rates. Storage lockers and units of all sizes, guarded by friendly, orange, roll-up garage-style doors, which were all securely locked and inaccessible behind a tall fence and computerized gate.

Soren scowled at the access panel, shoved wet hair out of his eyes and pressed the Call button. Nothing happened. He punched some random numbers. Nothing. He rattled the gate. Still nothing. With his luck, 24/7 security meant there was a video camera somewhere taping him and in the morning someone might or might not scan the tape for unusual happenings.

"Shit."

He stabbed at a few more numbers. Maybe there was an intruder alert and overweight security guards would come running. He waited, shivering, his arms wrapped around him, thoroughly miserable.

"Hello?" he yelled. "Hello?" Nothing. Instead, he heard what sounded like a car approach. "God damn."

Since this was obviously not his lucky day, he wasn't about to take his chances on the side of the road, hoping for a friendly old lady taking pity on him and driving him to the nearest police station. It had to be pissed off Timoteo and bleached Eleoterio in their van.

Running was out of the question. And the only lit place he'd finally found was surrounded by barren, muddy fields. No shrubs were in sight.

He eyed the chain-link fence topped with barbed wire. He frantically pushed more numbers and the Call button, then did the next best thing. He scaled the gate, which was easier said than done, and mostly fell on the other side, landing in an ungraceful heap, jarring his hip and driving spears of agony down into his leg and up his spine. His vision grayed out. Reflexive tears leaked from the corners of his eyes, mingling with rain water. He panted through the pain, afraid to pass out.

On his back, without the breath to curse, he thought he heard a van, car, whatever, approach. He rolled to his side, struggled to his feet and by the time the van crawled by the gate—driver and passenger doing their best to see past the sheets of rain—Soren had limped around the back of the one-story administrative building. He found the door marked Security just as two uniformed men spilled out of it.

"Hold it right there, buddy!" The burlier, shorter of the two security guards had one hand over a giant-sized canister of pepper spray on his belt.

"Freeze, punk." The other guard had his impressive looking black and yellow Taser stun gun aimed at Soren.

These guys meant business. And they seemed a tad bit trigger happy. Soren didn't move a muscle. He grumbled. It was entirely unfair that he stood in the lashing rain, the wind buffeting him, while the guards didn't venture past the building's overhang.

"Had trouble reading the sign, huh?"

"What part of 24/7 security made you think you could waltz right in and—"

"I wasn't breaking in. I—"

"Ah." The guy with the pepper spray relaxed his stance, but his hands kept hovering over his defensive arsenal. "Forgot your access code, huh?"

"Yeah. And the key to the handcuffs." The guy with the stun gun scowled.

The other guard snickered.

"Listen. Really. I need—"

"Don't get smart with us, kid. We see the likes of you everyday. Where're your buddies?"

"I'm alone. I need—"

"Alone?" The stun gun guy scowled deeper. "You're stupider than you look. We've got state of the art security surveillance. We saw you mess with the access panel, too, punk."

Soren swore. What the fuck? They'd watched him. "Yeah, hello, I was—"

"This some sort of initiation?"

"You escape from somewhere?"

Yes, but Soren figured it was probably best not to mention that. "I had some trouble. I was—"

"Oh, you're in trouble all right." A broad grin split the guard's face. "Go ahead," he urged, "make my day." He jerked his Taser at Soren. "I've been meaning to try this thing out. Run. Go for it."

"Jesus. You guys are fucking nuts. Will you call the freaking cops already?"

"Right."

"I think he's high," The man with the pepper spray said to his comrade, then turned towards Soren. "Had a bit much to smoke today, huh? Figured you could rip off Uncle Bob's and score some more ice, huh? You're not the first to try, buddy."

Soren didn't know why anyone would want to break into a

storage facility. He figured the stuff behind the orange roll-up doors had to be old junk that people didn't want cluttering their homes. No one in their right mind would store something valuable in a rented garage. But he was afraid if he voiced his opinion he'd get tasered for derogatory comments. Rent-a-cop two seemed to be itching for a reason to try out his oversized toy.

"It's raining, you know," Soren pointed out instead.

"Typhoon's coming in."

"Yeah, but you're not. We're not that dumb. You stay right there."

"Jesus. Come on, man. It's pouring."

"Tough shit. Should've dressed for the occasion."

"He did," Pepper Spray snickered, looking at the dangling handcuffs. After a quick exchange of meaningful eye contact and lip twitches with his partner, he slowly backed up and disappeared into the bowels of the small building. Presumably to call in real cops.

Soren hung his head. He was alive and out of sight; he couldn't ask for more. It wasn't as if he could get any wetter. Ten minutes wouldn't make much of a difference. He'd stand in the torrential rain and wait.

By the time the burly guard returned, Soren was beyond miserable. He was so cold he could barely control his shivering. He was wetter than he had ever been in his entire life—if that was possible—and ready to be stun-gunned and tasered just to get out of the rain and biting wind. On the upside, he was so numb he barely felt pain anymore.

The puddle he was standing in had risen to ankle-depth. The storage courtyard was slowly flooding.

There was a hushed but tense conversation taking place when Soren looked up. The guy with the pepper spray didn't look happy. "The cops are busy," he explained. "The streets are flooding and traffic lights are out. It'll take them a while to get here. What's your name, kid?"

"Soren."

"What kind of name is that?"

"What the hell is yours?"

"Watch it, pal."

"He's Flores." Pepper Spray jerked a thumb at his zealous co-worker, then introduced himself, "I'm Vicente Chargualaf."

Soren nodded.

"Your friends were at the gate," Chargualaf said. "Not too smart either. What is it with you guys and the Call button?"

Flores's face lit up. "We should let them in. I want to shoot this thing."

Soren's head jerked up. "No!"

Flores's eyes immediately narrowed with suspicion.

"They're not my friends," Soren explained. He had no idea, of course, if the men at the gate were indeed Timoteo and Eleoterio. Maybe the men at the gate were just two guys with a broken down car in need of assistance? He didn't want to take the risk. "They're dangerous," he growled and lifted his wrist with the handcuff dangling from it. "I was kidnapped. They're looking for me," he said.

"Yeah."

"Right."

Neither Flores, whose arms had to be getting tired holding up his massive weapon, nor the burlier Chargualaf looked impressed or in the slightest way convinced.

"Got a last name?" Flores inquired with a sneer.

Soren hesitated. "Yes. And it's none of your business." He had no desire to end up in his father's clutches again or to hand himself over to the FBI just yet. He needed to sort some things out first. He needed Mason and his no-nonsense advice. But he didn't know how to get in contact with Mason. During all their time on the Sprite, Soren hadn't seen any need to inquire about a phone number. Mason was probably in the phone book, though. He was surely in the phone book. He had a business after all. Or Soren could just have them call the cops.

"Call the cops again. Stoney Ward, he's a cop. He knows me. He's looking for me."

"I knew it!" Immediately Flores was on guard again, widening his stance and correcting his aim.

Damn.

"Kidnapped, huh?" His eyes narrowed.

Exasperated, Soren yanked up his shirt and exposed bruised skin. "You think I did this to myself?"

Flores's expression clearly said he wouldn't put a self-inflicted injury past Soren. Anything to rob Uncle Bob's.

Chargualaf asked, "You worth something?"

"To the police, yes. I'm ... a witness. I saw something I shouldn't have." Soren tried his best to look young and vulnerable. Soaking wet and shivering, that wasn't too hard to portray. He had to work, though, to keep his impatience out of his voice. "Listen, you don't have to trust me. Lock me up somewhere. Stoney Ward, I swear, he'll come and get me." He paused before offering what would hopefully win Flores and Chargualaf over. "You'll be doing the police a service."

Over the wind and rain, Soren didn't hear what the men started discussing, but their conversation was animated. He ducked his head in an effort to keep the rain off his face and hunched his shoulders. He'd given up on his hair. Shoving it out of his eyes was a losing battle. Maybe Mason was right, and he needed a haircut. Mason was right about so many other things, odds were he had the right idea about the hair, too.

"Huh?" He opened his eyes and blinked rain out of his lashes.

"Inside," Flores repeated with a jerk of his chin in the direction of the back door.

Inside turned out to be a windowless office, overcrowded with monitors, a high-tech, sleek computer, massive amounts of paperwork and files cramped into an in-box and out-box or teetering precariously on shelves, an antique rotary dial phone and three rickety chairs that looked immensely uncomfortable. It reeked of Chinese take-out.

"Sit. And don't move a muscle."

Soren obediently dropped into the chair Flores pointed to. Pain shot across his hip and pelvis. He squirmed on his seat until he found a somewhat comfortable position, half off and half on the chair.

Flores had his narrowed eyes and Taser on him and smirked. "Hemorrhoids?"

"Wanna have a look?" Soren shot back. He was fairly miserable. His T-shirt clung to him like second skin, which did nothing to help him stay warm. His pants were so thoroughly soaked, they weighed a ton and dragged across his already bruised hip—it didn't help that he wasn't wearing underwear. His toes could swim inside his worn tennis shoes, but at least the water could drain through the holes in them.

Chargualaf was on the phone. "What was that cop's name again?"

"Stoney Ward."

Chargualaf nodded. He had the phone wedged between his right ear and shoulder. "What's his rank? Ward. He got a rank?"

"Uh. I don't know."

"His precinct?"

Soren hesitated. Had Stoney told him? Something about teenage delinquents ... He was fairly sure Stoney was a plainclothes officer, but he really had no clue. Stoney was a cop, that was all he'd needed to know at the time. "Not sure."

Flores was immediately suspicious again. "Don't know. Not sure. How the hell do we know this Ward is a cop?"

"Jesus! Ask him for his badge when he gets here."

"Don't get smart with me, pal." Flores broke into a wide grin. "I'm still hoping to test my baby"—he gently caressed his stun gun with his free hand—"on you."

Soren took a deep breath, when a thought occurred to him. "Do you ever check on the people who press the Call button? You know, let them in maybe?"

Flores and Chargualaf looked at him with wide-eyed disbelief.

"Guess not." He fixed his eyes on the puddle he was creating and prayed for a quick pick-up.

26

"My ass hurts." Stoney slid farther down on his orange plastic chair and stretched out his long legs. It was well past midnight, and he was fast nearing the end of his patience. He had had all the hospital coffee and food one person could stand and his back was begging him to exchange the hard plastic chair for a bed.

He was about to call out to Mason who was chatting with the security guard on night shift when his cell phone started vibrating against his waist. He clipped it from his belt and frowned at the display. The precinct was looking for him.

"Yeah? Ward." He frowned. "Who?" He sat up straighter and grinned at Mason who was bidding the security guard good night. "No shit."

A call was routed his way and some guy described Soren in great detail. Stoney accepted responsibility for his pickup. "I'll be right there," he said and disconnected.

"Work?"

"No, some security guy at Uncle Bob's Storage. Seems they found something that belongs to you, and we're going to pick it up."

Mason gave his brother a blank look.

"Soren turned up." Stoney's grin threatened to unhinge his jaw as he clapped his brother on the back and steered him down the deserted hospital hallway. "Let's go. The black-and-whites can talk to the skipper when he wakes up. We need to haul ass, collect your boy, and hole up somewhere until this storm is over."

"He's not my boy," Mason scoffed and lengthened his stride.

Oh yes, he was. Stoney couldn't help but grin like a loon. He'd seen the hope and relief and concern flash across his twin's face.

"He's not," Mason said.

Stoney just nodded then made his way out to the Jeep.

Navigating flooded streets in a torrential rainstorm took all his concentration—it didn't help that his Jeep was almost immediately plastered with shredded palm fronds and banana leaves—lovingly referred to as storm salad—and an assortment of trash that reduced poor visibility even further. By the time they reached Uncle Bob's, Mason had succumbed to his exhaustion and was asleep in the backseat.

At the gate Stoney contemplated his next move. Squinting at the computerized access panel through a window he refused to lower didn't get him in contact with the people inside. He honked his horn several times and waved at the security camera mounted near the gate. As an afterthought, he took his shield out of his back pocket and held it up against the windshield.

Nothing happened.

Mason didn't stir, which began to bother Stoney. True, the

man was an ex-Ranger, able to sleep anywhere, but the horn should have woken him up.

With a sigh, Stoney fished his cell phone out of his pocket, called information, got the number for Uncle Bob's and called there.

"Will you let me in already?" he barked at the guy who answered the phone. For good measure, he honked his horn.

"And you would be?"

"Stone Ward. We spoke, uh,"—he glanced at his wrist watch—"an hour or so ago. I'm here to pick up Soren. You know, the cranky redhead."

There were noises and mumbling coming over the line as if someone had his hand over the receiver of the phone. Then, "How do we know you're really him?"

"Who else would it be?"

"You tell us, pal." A new voice.

"I tell you what," Stoney began patiently. "I will wait two minutes for this gate to open. If it does not open, I will drive home, get a cold beer and enjoy TV while the electricity is still on. Feel free to keep Soren. I'll send the FBI in for him later."

"The FBI?"

Stoney nodded. "That's what I said."

"Is he dangerous?"

Stoney thought that over. "I don't think so. He's got a bit of a temper, though. Swears a lot."

Again there was rustling and mumbling coming over the line, before the first guy came back on. "Give us your shield number and information. We'll call it in and verify you are who you say you are. Just wait. Don't go."

He sounded a bit desperate and Stoney complied.

It took three songs, four cheesy radio commercials and a weather update before the gate swung open.

Stoney angled his Jeep next to the security entrance in such a way that he only had to dash two, maybe three feet through the torrential downpour, but he still got soaked. Cursing loudly, he stood in a narrow hallway and shook himself like a dog.

"Yo," he called out.

"You Ward?"

Stoney nodded—what were the odds of someone else walking in off the street?—and took in the pair before him. Middle-aged, receding hairlines, in wrinkled uniforms, enough pepper spray and stun power between them to take out a small riot. The taller one had fever bright eyes and a nervous hand hovering over his Taser. The shorter one was a bit heavy around the middle. Together they frowned at Stoney expectantly.

"Yes." He produced his shield, handed it over and peered down the hallway. "Where's Soren?"

"Right here."

Stoney peered over the shoulder of the shorter guy and caught Soren limping down the hallway toward him. He was as dirty as a dog romping through a muddy field. He looked like he'd been the losing party in a big fight. There was a handcuff dangling from his left wrist and blood had soaked into his shirt. All in all, he looked like shit. But the expression on his face—the visible part that wasn't obscured by a tangled red mass—was pure relief.

"Yo," Stoney greeted. "You okay?"

"Yeah."

Stoney raised his brows, but didn't bother replying the obvious. "Great. Let's get the hell out of here." Stoney waved at the guards who shuffled their feet and fidgeted. "Bye guys. Thanks for keeping him."

"What about the reward?"

"The what?" Stoney glanced from the guards to Soren who had the nerve to look him straight in the eye and shrug. "Right. The reward. I tell you what." He took his wallet out of his back pocket again and riffled through an assortment of old receipts, notes, and wallet-sized photos until he found what he was looking for. "Call this guy in the morning. Nuh, make that late afternoon." He handed Kaoru's business card to the taller guy with the nervously twitching hand. "He'll take care of you."

Without so much as a glance back at the hired help, Stoney

turned and shoved the door open to the outside. He shrugged at the inevitable, nodded at Soren, and dashed into the rain and to the driver side of his Jeep.

Soren followed less nimbly. He was soaked to the bone by the time he climbed into the passenger side.

And then Stoney saw it again, that expression of hope and relief and concern all rolled into one, only this time it spread across Soren's face as he took in Mason still sound asleep in the backseat, still snoring.

Soren ducked his head and reached up to rub his forehead. "I think I remember him saying something about wanting to kick my ass if we got out of that stupid storm room."

"Yeah," Stoney drawled. "He might have mentioned something along those lines a time or two tonight. You sure you're okay? You don't look okay."

"I'm fine, just ... sore."

"Need a doc?"

"No."

"Okay then." Stoney gave Soren credit for sitting up straight. There was something obviously wrong with his hip or his leg. He gestured for Soren's hand and used a key on his key ring to free the redhead from his dangling handcuff.

"Let's get the hell out of here." He steered them into the torrential downpour and flying debris. The wipers did their thing as fast as they could, but it wasn't much help. After a long moment Stoney said, "I don't think you want me to drive you home, do you?"

Soren winced.

Stoney clenched his jaw and swallowed the first thing that threatened to spill over his tongue. Chances were, Soren knew perfectly well that James Buchanan was a poor excuse for a father. In the end, he decided on, "Mason was pretty worried about you. Kaoru, too. Why didn't you call?"

Soren hesitated.

"He is the FBI, you know."

"Exactly."

Stoney wasn't sure he understood, but he had a pretty good idea. Whatever else he'd done, James had managed to keep his son's loyalty intact.

"Where are we going?"

"There's someone who wants to meet you," Stoney said. "We were thinking about holing up at the Blue Heaven again, but you escaped from there once already," he let his voice trail off as he swerved to avoid a picnic table being blown across the street. "You're about to meet the toughest woman on the block. She'll fix you up with a shower and some food. I'd eat quickly," he advised and grinned at the soggy redhead next to him, "because Mason was pretty adamant about kicking your ass when he got a hold of you." Among other things, but Stoney didn't see the need to mention those. "Kaoru told him about the stash of pills in your room."

"Fuck."

Stoney grumbled and jerked the wheel. "Damn, I can't see a thing. Was that a tree we just ran over?"

27

They rode in companionable silence (Mason's snoring notwithstanding). Now and again Stoney cursed, often followed by the Jeep wildly swerving to avoid colliding with stray garbage cans rolling across the street or lawn furniture flying by.

Soren, thankful for the absence of questions and lectures, didn't care where they were driving until he recognized the outskirts of Santa Rita. Nestled across the slopes of Mount Alifan, the village was known for its spectacular views of Apra Harbor.

"You live around here?"

"Nope, but my mother does."

"Your mom?"

"Yes. Here we are."

It turned out that the brothers' boyhood home—despite its elevated location at the very end of a dead-end street—didn't offer any dazzling ocean views. Or a garage for that matter, which meant the men would have to sprint through the lashing wind and rain to the ornately carved front door.

"I wonder how long we would have to sit here before my mom comes out with rain gear." Stoney sighed wistfully.

Soren glanced from the solidly built and utterly unattractive, concrete, two-story family home to the man sitting next to him, back to the house. "You can't take me to your mom's."

"Why not?"

"Because she's your mom."

"Trust me, my mother can handle whatever trouble is following you. Besides." Stoney made a face and raked a hand through his dark hair. "My mom is a very tough woman to say no to, and she about had my hide when she found out about Mason and you."

Soren paled.

Stoney snickered. "The trouble you guys got yourselves into with your father," he clarified. "Let's get you inside, so she can fuss over you."

"What about Mason?"

"Oh, she'll fuss over him, too."

Soren rolled his eyes.

Stoney reached between the seats and shook his brother's leg. Mason swatted his hand away, which seemed to satisfy Stoney. "He's awake." He turned to Soren and jerked his chin in the direction of the house. "You first. You're slow."

"Wouldn't you want to be in front of me then?"

Stoney laughed. "Good point. Oh, hell, let's just go. It's only water."

The three of them dashed through the rain and predictably Stoney reached the front door first. "Yo," he called into the house, shaking rain from his hair and shoulders. "Mom?" He pulled Soren over the threshold and avoided his brother's eyes.

Mason had fallen asleep thinking they'd spend the night at the Blue Heaven Motel. Seeking refuge at their mother's would not have been an option on his list, which was why Stoney hadn't bothered waking him to discuss it. "Mom, we made it."

"I can tell." Mrs. George Ward—born George Barbara Susan Williams, named after an uncle who'd given his life in Pearl Harbor in 1941—appeared in the door off the kitchen. The rich aroma of hot chocolate followed her into the hallway. She smiled warmly and rose on her toes to greet her eldest with a kiss brushed over his wet cheek. She pulled Mason into a hug, released him, and held her hand out to Soren.

"Very nice to meet you, Soren. Welcome to my home. Just call me George."

Soren's polite "Thank you, ma'am" had Stoney looking at him with astonishment. Soren hadn't struck him as the type with respect for his elders.

"I've got soup, hot chocolate and warm towels for you boys," George said, ready to usher the men into the kitchen.

Mason snagged Soren's shirtsleeve and pulled him back. "We'll be right in, mom."

He waited until Stoney and his mother disappeared in the kitchen, before raking his eyes over Soren's disheveled form.

"You okay?"

"Yeah."

"As okay as you were last week?"

Soren frowned, then remembered. "You just want me to take my clothes off again."

Mason wrinkled his nose. "Damn right I do. You smell like a wet dog." That didn't stop him from running his hand down Soren's arm, though. "What happened?"

"The usual."

"Kaoru came for you. Your father, and I use that term loosely, said you'd left with Jolina."

Soren snorted. "Sure did. And her nutcase cousins." He gave Mason an abridged rundown of the events since they'd parted.

Mason swore.

Stoney, driven by curiosity, peeked around the corner. "Soup's ready."

George stepped into the hallway behind her son. "I'll get you boys some warm towels."

Mason waited until his mother was up the stairs and out of earshot to round on his brother. "I can't believe you called her."

"I didn't," Stoney snapped. "What, you think I'm nuts?" He scratched at the stubble on his chin. "Come on. You know as well as I do that I can't file a report with your name in it and not expect Mom to hear about it. That woman is better connected than Buchanan."

"What does she know?"

"Does it matter? Look at you." Stoney gestured at his brother, then waved at Soren. "You're both dead on your feet. And so am I for that matter. He can't walk straight and you—how many fingers am I holding up?" He held up his middle finger.

"Very mature, Stone."

Stoney shrugged. "Man, it's been a long day. Just have some freaking soup, and we'll figure this out."

When George reentered the kitchen with three dryer-warmed towels in her hands, her sons were eating and Soren was sitting in front of a steaming mug of hot chocolate, his pale fingers curled around the mug, leaching the warmth from it.

George smiled at him and nodded at the hot chocolate he hadn't touched. "If you'd prefer, I could make you some hot tea," she offered.

"Oh, no, thank you, ma'am." He smiled back. "This is fine."

"Not a tea drinker?"

He made a face, and she laughed.

Stoney smiled. He'd known his mother would like Soren. She had a thing for strays. She was a great mom, Stoney thought with pride.

She was in her mid fifties. Fit. Athletic. Maybe a bit rounder around the middle than she preferred to be. Her hair was closely cropped, the mink brown not chemically enhanced. She had the same espresso-colored eyes as her sons, but life, three children and the premature death of a husband she'd dearly loved had etched fine lines and subtle wrinkles into her face. She was a no-nonsense kind of woman who didn't beat around the bush.

"So what kind of trouble can we expect?"

Mason glared at his brother before explaining what their situation seemed like.

"So this woman and her cousins might or might not be looking for you right now?"

Soren nodded.

"What about your father?"

"I doubt it. He wasn't expecting me back tonight. Unless they told him I'm gone, he wouldn't know."

Stoney's phone began to vibrate against his belt. He excused himself and stepped into the hallway. By the time he returned, his mother had cleared the table. She handed him a thermos.

"What's that?"

"Soup."

"I'm not leaving."

"Oh yes, you are. They wouldn't call you in unless they needed you. Storm's bad. Are they closing the roads?"

"Yes."

"They'll have a roadblock down at the intersection. I'll call and make sure they have the description of the van Soren gave us. We'll be fine, honey. Go to work."

Stoney grumbled. He'd meant what he'd told Soren, his mother was perfectly able to handle herself. Still, he didn't like the idea of leaving.

"Why don't you show Soren upstairs on your way out? I need to have a talk with your brother." She cupped his face in her hands and pulled him down for a kiss on the forehead. "Drive safely."

Stoney sighed. There was no arguing with his mother. He

waved at Soren and trudged into the hallway. "Come on, Red, I'll show you around. Guest bedroom used to be Mason's bedroom."

Soren followed obediently. He waited until they were upstairs to voice his concerns. "You can't leave me here with Mason and your mom."

Stoney smirked. He had a feeling that hadn't come out quite the way Soren had meant it. "Don't worry about it. She can handle trouble. She'll back up Mason. You're in great hands."

Soren didn't look convinced.

"Bedroom." Stoney opened a door, pointed. "Bathroom's in the back. Connects to the other bedroom. Relax. Between the two of them, they won't let anything happen to you."

"Uh huh."

"I mean it." Stoney went back downstairs and opened the front door. He groaned at the sight of the undiminished downpour. He'd be wet again before he reached his Jeep. Door in hand, towel slung over his shoulders, he turned and winked at the redhead. "You're perfectly safe."

"But—"

"Soren, she's a cop."

28

Still in the kitchen, George studied Mason from over the rim of her mug of hot chocolate. "You have that look on your face."

"I let him down."

"I can see how you'd think that."

Mason scowled at his mother. He'd completely underestimated The Smile. He'd done a lousy job of looking after Soren. Never mind that Kaoru's job description had been "keep him out of sight and sober," not "watch out for kidnappers."

"Did you see him?"

"I sure did." She smiled. "Caren Lund's son. I never thought I'd have him in my house."

Mason's scowl darkened. That was not what he'd meant and his mother knew it.

George put her mug down and leaned towards Mason. "Soren is a young man fully capable of making his own decisions, who ran away from you and returned home despite knowing what his father was capable of."

"Ran away from me," Mason pointed out, exasperated.

"Because you were lying down on the job?"

"Right."

George rolled her eyes. "That boy is a classic victim of family violence, downplaying what his father does, blaming his own behavior. The alcohol. The drugs. Even going back home, especially going back home. You know that."

Yes, Mason knew. Soren's unfailing loyalty to his father was just another sign of his dysfunctional upbringing.

"You can't blame yourself for his actions or what they set in motion."

Mason scrubbed a hand down his face and sighed. His mother wasn't helping. He should have kept a better eye on Soren. True, he'd only been charged with protecting the redhead from his father, but he should have known to protect Soren from himself. He'd failed. Period.

"You should check on him," George said as she pushed away from the table. "I'll be in my room if you need anything."

Mason nodded, pulled his phone from the waistband of his jeans and called Kaoru. By the time his friend was done chewing him out, the National Weather Service had downgraded the typhoon warning to a tropical storm warning, not that that changed very much. Monsoon-like torrential rains were still a major cause for concern across the island. It was only the widespread flooding, the inevitable loss of electricity and the havoc both would cause that convinced Kaoru to trust Mason with Soren until daybreak.

"You're mine for a few more hours," Mason whispered as he marched from the kitchen and climbed the stairs to the second floor. He rapped his knuckles against his old bedroom door before walking inside. He had no intention of waiting for permission to enter the guest room or of respecting Soren's privacy.

"We need to talk," he said, but the room was empty. His concern and anger were immediate. Christ, he couldn't leave the kid alone for a minute! He stood with his fists clenched at his side when the noise of running water splashing into a sink registered. The door to the small bathroom that connected his room to Stoney's was ajar. Mason stepped closer.

Soren stood bent over the sink, his back to the door and Mason. His hair was wet, his torso bare, a towel clung to his hips.

Mason's eyes homed in on the red welts and livid bruises marring the redhead's pale back and shoulders. With an angry growl, he shoved the bathroom door open, startling Soren. His anger must have been apparent, because the redhead took a wary step back and bumped into the sink as Mason stalked across the threshold. Mason ground his teeth and grabbed a wrist. "You," he hissed.

He yanked the redhead across the bathroom, gave the door an angry nudge with his boot—it slammed shut—and pushed Soren up against it none too gently. He crowded the younger man. Hands on either side of Soren's wet head, close enough that his thumbs could slide into the dark red hair that clung to Soren's neck and shoulders. He pushed his right thigh between Soren's legs, grinding hard muscle against Soren's groin.

Soren's eyes sparked jade fire. His chin rose. The hands at his sides balled into fists, but he didn't say anything. Mason shifted his weight, which brought all of him in contact with Soren's body. Because of their difference in height, Mason's jean-clad erection pressed hard against Soren's lower abdomen.

The widening of Soren's green eyes was the only outward sign of his surprise.

Mason's mouth came down hard on Soren's, crushing lips against teeth. It was all there in his bruising kiss and roaming hands: his hunger, his anger and his desperation to touch Soren, to make sure the redhead was okay.

"God help me, but I want you." Mason ground his teeth. "Here and now. Against this door."

Soren wrapped his hands around Mason's waist, fisting the back of Mason's shirt. He didn't shrink back, didn't protest, if anything, he came even closer, apparently not minding Mason's rough need.

"No," Mason whispered as he took a step away from Soren. "I won't hurt you," he said. It wasn't an empty vow; no meaningless, clichéd phrase he uttered in the heat of the moment. His heart lurched under the weight of its significance. He wanted to help Soren, protect him. Keep him.

"It's not what I want. I—" Mason forced out a harsh breath and bridged the distance between them with a quick step. He lowered his head, touching his forehead to Soren's. "I need to know you're safe. The idea that he ... touched you ... that I wasn't there to protect you ..." Mason's voice trailed off as he gently brushed a thumb over an angry red welt crossing Soren's shoulder. He slowly lowered his mouth to the red skin and laid a kiss over the welt. He nuzzled Soren's wet hair, inhaling the scent of his mother's fancy guest soap, and brushed his lips over the shell of Soren's ear. His hand slid up the column of Soren's throat and felt the frantically beating pulse there. Soren trembled.

Mason blinked and focused on the eyes looking up at him. Under golden lashes the green was a brilliant halo around the dilated pupils. That wasn't fear looking up at him. It was arousal.

Mason's hand slid through Soren's wet hair and his mouth came down on Soren's once more. Soren opened his mouth and Mason's tongue took full advantage of the opportunity, delving into the hot moisture.

Soren's hands came up and his arms slid around Mason's neck. His eyes closed, and Mason discovered that Soren's eyelids were also sprinkled with freckles.

Urgent, hungry need slammed into Mason like a vicious fist to the gut and the moan that spilled past his lips was part pain, part arousal. The guttural sound made Soren's eyes fly open.

Mason slid his lips down Soren's throat, across his collarbone, the angry welt raised by a belt, the curve of his shoulder. His hands roamed over Soren's heaving chest. For once Mason did not feel as if he was in control. His hands slid over Soren's body, touching him the way he'd wanted for so long. When he encountered Soren's towel, Mason tore his mouth away from Soren's throat. There would be no going back if he took the towel from around Soren's waist. He stopped, but kept his hand on the towel.

"You're not stopping now," Soren said breathlessly.

"I should."

Soren reached down to where Mason's hand held the towel. Without breaking eye contact, he moved Mason's hand away and let the towel fall to the floor. Soren grinned, and Mason slid his hands over the swell of Soren's ass, pulling the redhead closer. Soren's throaty whimper fuelled his desire.

"Fifteen minutes," he breathed against Soren's neck. He stepped away from the door and dragged Soren with him. He fumbled with the doorknob and cursed. "Maybe twenty," he said, then pulled Soren toward the bed.

29

Soren's back hit the bed, and Mason was able to get a good look at the bruises that marred Soren's beautiful body. He swore under his breath then slid down next to Soren and bathed the bone-deep bruising over his hip with feather-light kisses. Mason's lips traveled across the flat of Soren's stomach to his navel. He pressed his mouth to the small indentation and let his tongue explore the shallow depths. He followed the trail of fine red hairs down to the base of Soren's cock.

Soren's eyes widened and his right hand came up, touching Mason's shoulder, then sliding through his hair. Mason smiled up at him and pushed his mouth over Soren's lean shaft.

Soren felt his cock throb and grow as it slid past Mason's lips. His head fell back onto the pillow, and his eyes closed. Each swipe of Mason's tongue was an electric shock that surged through Soren's system, leaving his nerves singed and his muscles trembling. Then Mason withdrew.

Bewildered, Soren opened his eyes to see Mason standing over him. Their eyes locked, then Mason began to undress with slow but deliberate movements until he stood naked at the foot of the bed.

Mason was more intimidating with his clothes off than with his clothes on. Now there was no mistaking the bulk of him for anything but muscle. His shoulders seemed broader, his waist narrower. Or it could have been Soren's angle and the fact that Mason was towering over him. Judging from Mason's smug expression, he very much enjoyed Soren's eyes on him.

Soren drank in the sight of the man. Mason's short, dark hair wasn't as neat as usual. Soren wanted to run his fingers through the dark patch of hair that nestled between Mason's nipples and trailed downward, dividing his stomach, until it met another dark patch of hair and feathered out across his powerful thighs.

"Like what you see?"

Soren lowered his gaze to Mason's erection and smirked. "Nice equipment."

Mason laughed. He crawled on top of Soren, reaching hungrily, running his hands up Soren's legs and lean torso. He lapped at a small, pale nipple that responded eagerly. He buried his nose in the hair at the nape of Soren's neck before moving on to Soren's mouth.

They kissed as if kissing alone would satiate their need. When they broke apart, Soren panted.

Mason took his muscled weight off Soren and stretched for the nightstand. "Roll over."

Soren turned as Mason exhaled what sounded suspiciously like a very vulgar, angry curse at the sight of abuse across the redhead's back.

"You're not going back," he growled, silently vowing to throttle The Smile the next time they met. "What the hell did he do to you?"

"I don't have anywhere else to go," Soren pointed out quietly.

"There are options," Mason said, then slid his lips over the nape of Soren's neck, brushing wet strands of hair to the side. Having Soren move in with him was not one of those options, he told himself. Never mind that the kid was ten years his junior or that they had very little in common; it simply wouldn't be smart. Hormones were clouding his judgment.

He laid a gentle trail of kisses down Soren's back, avoiding welts and bruises and the occasional scrape, until he arrived at the valley of Soren's lower back, where fine red hairs tickled his lips. He hesitated.

Soren sat up. He plastered himself from hip to shoulder against Mason's front, then flexed his pelvis and wiggled his butt, which made Mason's hard cock slide between the soft mounds of his cheeks.

Mason let out a soft moan as he slid his hands around Soren's waist and took hold of Soren's erection.

"If you're not going to do me," Soren said, "I'll have to force myself on you. But I'd rather—" He exhaled a long groan when Mason's fingers closed around his engorged cock. The rough pad of Mason's thumb brushed over Soren's leaking head, and Soren went back down on all fours with Mason following behind, never letting go of Soren's hard shaft.

Mason settled against Soren's back, careful to brace most of his weight on his forearm. His fingers stayed curled around Soren's cock, working the hard shaft with rough, powerful strokes. His lips settled over the curve of Soren's shoulders. His own neglected cock pulsed against Soren's ass, finding a comfortable channel between cheeks that were clenching and unclenching in tandem with Mason's strokes.

Soren arched against him. He rolled his shoulders and flexed his pelvis, feeding more of himself into Mason's fist, pressing back against the heated flesh nestled between his buttocks, leaving very little doubt that he wanted this as much as Mason. He had his face turned into the pillow to catch his moans.

Mason pulled his hand away and settled his weight along Soren's legs. His large hands gripped Soren's waist. He slid the rough stubble of too many days without a shave over the swell of Soren's ass and the back of his thighs. He followed the scrape of his beard with his tongue and his lips.

Soren clutched the sheets. He nearly came off the bed when Mason leaned in and swiped his tongue over the tight opening he found between freckled butt cheeks.

Mason pushed his tongue inside. Soren was warm and clean, pulsing against him. Excited by the thought of burying himself inside that tight heat, Mason nearly came. He plunged his tongue deeper. Soren started to whimper.

Mason stopped and reached around Soren's bruised hip. His hand slid over the engorged head of Soren's cock.

Soren's throaty pleas were Mason's undoing. Lust threatened to take his resolve to go slow, to mind the aches, bruises, and Soren's inexperience. But greed outweighed his lust. He wanted to hear Soren moan, wanted his name to fall from the kid's mouth. He wanted Soren senseless with need. Above all, though, he wanted the young man under his hands and tongue to remember his first time with a man as pleasurable enough to ask for more.

"You're going to like this," he promised, fumbling for the years-old bottle of lubricant he'd retrieved from the nightstand.

He slid one lubricated finger into the depth of Soren's ass. Soren tensed, relaxed and rocked back against Mason. He squirmed against the finger impaling him.

"Fuck me," Soren whispered.

Mason ground his teeth and slid another finger into Soren's eager hole, stretching it, lubricating it. He pushed in deeply.

Soren moaned.

Mason withdrew his fingers, then quickly searched out the condom he kept in his wallet. Sheathed in latex, he came back to the bed. He pressed his thumb against Soren's eager hole before sliding it in and out of the tight opening

"Please," Soren moaned.

Mason replaced his thumb with the length of his aching cock. Soren tensed, then exhaled and his body relaxed.

Mason slowly rocked in and out of Soren's ass, mindful of the bruises under his hands and the constricting tightness gripping him like a vise. But Soren had other ideas, thrusting back eagerly as Mason slid into him, setting a quicker pace, asking for more than gentle lovemaking.

In the end, Soren was on his hands and knees again, his face buried in the pillow, his stiff cock swinging underneath him, slapping against his belly, while Mason relentlessly drove into his body.

Mason felt rather than heard Soren's cry of completion, the redhead's body clenching around him. Pumping once, twice more, Mason's shaft swelled and he let the orgasm wash over him, following his lover over the edge with his own hoarse cry.

Sweaty and exhausted, the two men dropped on the bed.

"That was freaking intense," Soren mumbled after a long moment of drowsy silence. He cracked one eye open and grinned at Mason. "Best twenty minutes ever."

Mason laughed softly. He rolled to his side and pushed himself into a sitting position. He had a feeling they'd go their separate ways come morning and looked down at the sweaty redhead to commit his sharp Nordic features to memory. The narrow face. The long nose. The prominent cheekbones and strong jaw. The mouth that was too wide, but very kissable. The freckles that dusted his forehead, the bridge of his nose, his eyelids and pretty much the rest of him down to his toes. He reached out and raked his fingers through Soren's copper hair. The unruly waves and tufts and cowlicks softened the sharp angles of Soren's face.

Uneasy about the sudden warmth that spread through his belly, Mason snatched his hand away. As much as he liked to think they could make it work, dragging the redhead into a relationship wouldn't be fair. Mason figured Soren probably wouldn't see it that way, but Soren had to give life on his own a go before committing to someone else.

    But until the storm let up, Mason had Soren with him. As much as he thought he should sleep in his twin's old room, he couldn't bring himself to leave Soren alone. Bad things happened when he did. Before he slipped off to sleep, he protectively pulled Soren against him. Tonight, Soren was his.

30

Soren dozed fitfully. He was tired and sore, but restful sleep eluded him. He couldn't stop thinking about what he'd done, what they'd done. He'd suspected sex with Mason would be different—for obvious reasons—but he hadn't been prepared for it to be life-altering. He knew, as he lay sprawled under the quilt next to Mason's warm, hard body, that his life had been changed irrevocably. Mason had done something to him that went beyond a simple broadening of his sexual horizon. Now all Soren had to do was figure out what to do with that change.

Mason, no doubt, would make his life more complicated and Soren didn't know if he could handle any more complications. At the very least, though, he figured, having discovered his latent gayness would make the break with his father that much easier. He wouldn't have to move out. James would kick him out and disown him in a heartbeat. It wouldn't be quite that pretty or painless, Soren knew, but the end result would be the same.

In the past, James had thrown money at the mistresses of his trophy sons, but Soren couldn't imagine his father financing a gay lover. He rolled out from under Mason's heavy arm and pushed at the sleeping body. "Did he offer you money to make you go away?"

Mason jerked awake.

"He offered you money, didn't he?" Soren pressed. "My father," he added when all he got from Mason was a blank expression.

"Yes."

"A lot of money?"

"Yes."

"Do you need money? I mean you live on this huge boat. You consult with the feds. You own half a business. You have money, don't you?"

Mason propped himself up against the headboard. "Not the kind your father offered."

"Were you tempted?"

"No."

Soren nodded and shifted his weight. He was trying to find a comfortable position. His hip was throbbing. His bones ached. He turned on his stomach, decided against that, turned on his side and away from Mason, then scooted back and settled most of himself along the length of Mason's legs, soaking up his warmth.

Mason was one of the few people he knew who didn't seem intimidated by his father, which made Soren wonder what kind of man Mason's father had been. "Tell me about your father."

Mason slid down under the quilt and made himself comfortable against Soren. He draped his arm across Soren's flank and splayed his hand across Soren's flat belly, his fingertips brushing coarse pubic hair. He pushed his nose into Soren's hair and rested his chin against Soren's shoulder.

"He must have died before you were born." He sighed wistfully. "I don't like to talk about my father."

Soren could understand that, but Mason must have had a great father. There was a photograph of the man in Mason's stateroom. He had his arm around a young Mason in the picture, and there were smiles on both their faces. The pride and love between them was evident.

"He was killed by a man who enjoyed beating his wife and kids," Mason said, his voice flat and emotionless.

"I'm sorry."

"He was a cop. He was on duty." Mason's voice grew softer. "It was a domestic disturbance. The guy came at him with a baseball bat. He landed one good blow."

Soren held his breath.

Mason's arms tightened around Soren in a fierce hug. "That's why there's no way in hell I'd take your father's money," he said fervently. "Sooner or later, it would be blood money." He slid his fingers over the bloody furrow along Soren's forearm and Soren swore he felt the man growl low in his throat. "Your father has been buying people for so long, he's forgotten that lives are not a commodity that can be bought and sold."

Soren didn't answer. His father's abrasive nature, the abuse, the money that bought friends and made friends disappear—it was an unfortunate part of his life the way his fair complexion was a part of his life. So he stayed out of the sun and avoided his father as best he could.

"Your dad. Your mom. Stoney. Cops, all of them. How come you're not one? Could it be that you're a bit like me? Bucking the trend?"

Mason grunted. "You wish. I'm nothing like you, kid."

Soren made a face. He wouldn't mind a grown-up sounding nickname. "How old are you anyway?"

"Ten years and fifty-three days older than you."

Soren did his best imitation of a Mason grunt. "Haven't thought about that at all, have you?" He could feel Mason's answering grin against his neck and shook his head.

"I did follow in my father's footsteps. I became a Ranger," Mason said softly after a few moments, nuzzling the back of Soren's neck. "I'll be right back."

Soren groaned when Mason's warmth disappeared and tendrils of cool night air slipped under the blanket. How could this feel so right after such a short amount of time? The man was a major pain, but in his unapologetic and unflinchingly honest way, Mason had expected more of him. And he'd expected Soren to expect more of himself and for himself. He didn't make Soren feel like a louse for tolerating abuse in exchange for paid bills and a roof over his head. He didn't dwell on Soren's mistakes or use past stupidity to predict future foolishness and an inability to make better decisions.

Mason had faith in him.

Soren groaned and buried his head in the pillow. And what had he done with his first chance to prove he'd learned something on the Sprite? He'd wasted it on a bottle of champagne, Jolina and chemical oblivion.

He needed to redeem himself. He needed to prove that the faith placed in him wasn't misplaced. He needed to make this a change for the better.

"You need to sleep," Mason said and slipped back into bed next to Soren. He slid his hands underneath the quilt and pulled Soren up against his chest. His mouth descended on Soren's, his tongue slipping inside with gentle insistence. Then, as quickly, as he'd started, he pulled away. "I need to sleep."

Soren smiled. He let himself be tucked against Mason's side and finally gave in to his body's need for rest.

31

Soren woke with a start around 4 a.m. One minute he was blissfully asleep, the next his body revolted and demanded his attention. He groaned and pressed his face back into the pillow, but it was a futile effort. His head was pounding. He was thirsty. He needed a drink of water. It would take him two minutes, he figured. Three at the most. But it would require movement, and he loathed the thought of making a single muscle in his body work—mostly because they all seemed to be sore and aching. The pounding behind his temples, though, didn't go away, and he was actually drooling into his pillow at the thought of a tall, cool glass of water.

Resigned, Soren held his breath and rolled out from under

Mason's heavy arm and the covers, and was rewarded with instant gooseflesh and a dull throb across his right hip. He slipped out of bed and padded naked, on silent feet, into the bathroom.

He felt around in the dark until he found the sweatpants George had left out for him before his shower. Although he couldn't see, he peered at the mirror and finger combed his hair. He pulled the medicine cabinet open and ran his hands over the contents, searching for prescription bottles. He found a manicure kit, adhesive tapes, a bottle that could be rubbing alcohol or peroxide, wrinkled tubes of cream and something he couldn't quite identify. It wasn't that he'd expected black-market drugs, but a woman of George's caliber—active and over 50—had to have some prescription pain killers. Didn't she?

He groaned just as his fingers encountered a small bottle of pills. Generic drugstore aspirins weren't his first choice, but they'd do. He shook a few tablets into his hand. He wasn't sure how many to take, but figured two wouldn't cut it, so he swallowed four and grimaced at the taste they left on his tongue.

He hurried to pull on his sweatpants and snuck out into the hallway and down to the kitchen. The house was quiet. The only sounds came from the ticking of a clock in the living room and the force of the rain against the windows and sides of the house. It was colder downstairs. So much so, Soren wondered if a window had been left open. He shook his head at the thought. George didn't strike him as a woman who left windows open during a typhoon.

Chilled air washed over him when he opened the refrigerator. He shivered. His cock and balls actually drew back looking for warmth as he lifted the orange juice out of the refrigerator.

"Hello, Soren," a voice drawled close to his ear.

"Fuck," he sputtered and nearly dropped the juice. "Jolina."

Slowly Soren turned to find Jolina standing behind him, a gun pointed at his face. He ground his teeth and a muscle jumped in his jaw. He'd wondered why he'd allowed himself to be caught in her web of alcohol, drugs and sex. Why hadn't he fought his father's ridiculous notion that bedding Jolina would be good for business? He wondered no more. She was a terrorist and as dangerous as the weapon in her hand, he knew that now. But a few weeks ago, all he'd seen was her small, perfect body, the roundness of her breasts—at the moment not covered very well by her wet silk blouse—the fullness of her lips and her beautiful hair.

"Surprise," she said.

"How did you find me?"

She shrugged and closed the gaping refrigerator door, plunging them into darkness. A moment later she turned on the light over the stove and waved Soren to a chair, which he ignored. "Your father was quite helpful. And pretty pissed." Her eyes traveled over the signs of James's last fit of temper across Soren's shoulders. Something behind Soren caught her attention for a moment. "Eleoterio is pretty pissed off, too."

Indeed he was. And quick on his feet. Eleoterio was in front of Soren before Jolina had ended her sentence. His backhand lashed across Soren's face. His fist to the stomach drove the air out of Soren's lungs and brought the redhead to his knees. Unlike James, who accompanied his abuse with a tirade, Eleoterio remained quiet.

He didn't give Soren the chance to wake the house either. He crouched over the redhead, all but sitting on his chest, pressing him to the kitchen floor with a knee across his windpipe.

"Don't kill him yet," Jolina said.

Soren struggled, but Eleoterio simply increased the pressure of his knee until Soren gave up and lay still. He was desperate for air. The throbbing behind his temples had escalated to a full blown migraine complete with nausea—or that could have been a side effect of the gut punch. His vision wavered. Fuck, he was going to die in borrowed, oversized sweatpants on George's kitchen floor.

"Wait until Timoteo comes back," Jolina instructed. She

crouched down next to Soren and with the muzzle of her gun pushed some hair out of his face. "He went upstairs to make sure we're not interrupted."

"Bitch," Soren spat.

Jolina snarled, got to her feet and drove a heeled foot into Soren's side. She flung her hair over her left shoulder and paced across the room, before she was in control enough to lean over Soren again. "Look who's talking," she said. "I'm not the one taking it up the ass, baby. And we both know how you like that."

Eleoterio raised his dark brows and smirked down at Soren. "You're so fucked."

Mason lay awake in bed, his head pillowed on his arm, waiting for Soren to return. He'd heard the redhead rummage through the medicine cabinet on a futile search for extra-strength painkillers. Or any other extra-strength drug, Mason suspected. They'd have to do something about the redhead's propensity to self-medicate when all this was over.

He yawned and raked a hand through his hair. He ran his fingers over the stitches holding his scalp together and cursed The Smile. He shook his head to dispel thoughts he didn't feel like entertaining at four in the morning and froze when he heard booted footfalls.

He slid out of bed and reached for his gun holster in the nightstand drawer. As quietly as possible he checked the magazine, then hit the redial button on his cell phone. He didn't wait for Kaoru to pick up. He dropped the phone on the unmade bed, didn't like its luminescent glow in the darkness, and shoved it under the bed instead. If chaos ensued, Kaoru could still hear.

He groped for his clothes on the chair next to the bed and pulled his black briefs over his hips. He stepped into the bathroom just as Timoteo gently pushed the bedroom door open all the way. Mason crossed the small bathroom, made sure the door to the adjacent bedroom was only ajar and stepped into the bathtub. He flattened himself against the tiles and waited.

Timoteo, who found an empty bedroom that should obviously have been occupied, followed the path Mason had lain. He looked into the bathroom, noticed the other door ajar and cursed under his breath. Interested only in his pursuit, he walked into the bathroom, eyes on the second door, and right past Mason. He brought his gun up and reached for the doorknob, peering into the darkness beyond. He listened intently and frowned when the rustle he heard didn't come from the empty bedroom but from behind him. He whirled directly into Mason's fist.

Surprise, momentum and a good amount of anger were enough to stun him. He fell back against the door.

Mason grabbed him by the shoulder, turned him and shoved his face into the doorframe. Dazed, Timoteo let out a groan as blood erupted from his nostrils.

"Not tonight," Mason growled. He took the gun from Timoteo's limp fingers, tossed it on the towel shelf and wrenched Timoteo's arm behind his back. But Timoteo took advantage of Mason's state of undress. He brought his booted foot down on Mason's unprotected toes, yanked his arm free then turned and sprang at Mason like a rabid cat. They crashed against the sink, sending toothbrushes, soap and an assortment of bathroom articles flying. They grappled for the gun in Mason's hand, but it was a short struggle.

Half dressed or not, Mason outweighed Timoteo and towered over him. A well-placed punch had Timoteo doubled over. A knee jerk upward had him flying back against the wall behind him. Blood gushing from his nose splattered the tiles. Mason wrapped his thick fingers around Timoteo's throat, threatening to crush his windpipe and Adam's apple in his grip.

"Son of a bitch," Mason hissed as he dragged the smaller man out of the cramped bathroom and into the bedroom, threw him against the wall and kept him there, letting him wheeze past the hand that strangled him. There was barely enough light to see by, but Mason could not miss the contempt glittering in Timoteo's eyes.

"Mason?" George called softly from the hallway.

Timoteo's eyes flickered. Mason recognized the look. He shook his head. With a cousin like Jolina, Timoteo should have known not to underestimate women. "I'm okay. This here dumb shit broke into the house of a cop. Got some handcuffs, Mom?"

George entered the bedroom, wearing a man's blue pin-striped pajamas and an expression that mirrored Timoteo's. Her smug grin, though, was backed up by the Beretta in her right hand and cuffs dangling from her other. "I got a closet, too, we can stuff him into."

"That'll work."

"Where's Soren?"

"Downstairs." Getting himself in trouble, no doubt. But Mason didn't voice his fear.

Even with two guns trained on him, Timoteo didn't see the need to cooperate. He spewed what in all likelihood amounted to foul curses in his native language and refused to move.

Mason would have none of that. Once the Filipino was handcuffed, he grabbed Timoteo by the hair and manhandled him into the walk-in closet George had judged a safe, temporary prison. He slammed the door closed, turned the key and took a deep breath.

"I called Kaoru," he said.

"I called the station."

Mason leaned down and kissed his mother on the cheek. "You're the best."

Timoteo threw himself at the closed door. It groaned, but held. George looked at her son. There was no way the closet door would withstand Timoteo for very long. Mason would have to go downstairs by himself.

"Be careful." She watched her son walk off and smiled. "And for God's sake, put some pants on."

32

Knowing when to shut up wasn't one of Soren's strengths. He figured it was some sort of an allergic reaction to bullying. It wasn't smart, but in the face of adversity he liked it better than cowering.

"Bite me," he said with his last breath. He gave up clawing at the leg across his throat and grabbed Eleoterio's foot instead. It was enough to unbalance the man. Soren reached around the leg that momentarily eased off his throat and grabbed Eleoterio's damp shirt. He yanked with what remaining strength adrenalin still gave him.

Eleoterio toppled. But he barely gave Soren time to fill his straining lungs with air. He yanked Soren up and threw him against the counter. The drying rack complete with mugs crashed into the sink. Appliances rattled. Soren groped blindly for anything to use in his defense as Eleoterio dragged him away and shoved him against the fridge. Colorful magnets went flying. The handle dug into Soren's back.

"Tonight you die," Eleoterio promised. He grabbed a fistful of red hair and jerked Soren around, sending him crashing into the cooking island.

"I don't think so." Soren's fingers curled around the handle of the tea kettle. He swung it like a baseball bat. And missed. Water splattered everywhere. "Fuck you."

Eleoterio lunged across the cooking island. He bore Soren down, and they rolled on the kitchen floor, trading punches and kicks. Soren came up short against the refrigerator. He grabbed one of the fallen magnets and hurled it at Eleoterio's face. It bounced off Eleoterio's forehead.

Jolina laughed.

Soren tried to shuffle out of her cousin's way, but the Filipino yanked him to his feet and tossed him back against the counter. "Fag," he snarled. He took a menacing step forward and slipped on the water spill. He staggered into the cooking island.

Soren took the chance he was offered. He hefted a black-and-white cookie jar off the counter and brought it down on the Filipino. The ceramic cow broke into pieces over Eleoterio's dark head.

Jolina's cousin looked stunned. His eyes glazed over and rolled into the back of his head as blood began to seep through his hair and drip over his face. He sank to his knees, then fell to the littered kitchen floor. He was either unconscious or dead—Soren didn't know which—before his head hit the floor.

"What have you done?" Jolina shrieked.

For once, Soren wisely kept his mouth shut and dashed from the room. He dove headlong into the dark dining room. A hail of bullets followed him. The door jamb splintered. Glass cabinet doors, George's black-and-white cow collection and crystal wine glasses exploded into tiny shards showering down on him.

"Fuck." Soren shook glass and cow parts out of his hair and hunkered down next to the buffet, flattening himself against the wall, hugging his legs to his chest.

"You're going to die, Soren. Come out and do it like a man."

Soren had no wish to die, manly, cowardly or otherwise. He crawled on all fours across the dining room, feeling his way between furniture. Unlike the kitchen, which was illuminated by the light over the stove, the dining room was pitch-black.

"For once in your life, stand up for yourself, Soren."

"What the fuck was I doing in there," Soren mumbled to himself.

"Son of a bitch." Jolina fired off a few more rounds, effectively destroying the rest of George's bovine collection. "You betrayed me."

"You used me," Soren called back. How many freaking bullets did her gun hold? How many had she wasted?

"Hey, you liked it. Oh, guess what I found."

"A conscience?"

She chuckled and flipped the light switch.

"Shit." Caught without anything shielding him, Soren threw himself at the only way out of the room: a door slightly ajar. As he tumbled towards the door he hoped it wasn't a closet he was diving into. It wasn't. He fell into the living room—upending potted peace lilies—and crashed into and over an armchair. He landed on his sore hip just as the lights flickered out.

Mason froze at the bottom of the stairs. He peered down the long dark hallway toward the living room, but didn't see a thing. Gun in both hands in front of him, a flashlight tucked into the waistband of his jeans, he crept into the kitchen. There was just enough pre-dawn light coming in through the window over the sink to recognize the large lump on the floor as a man—not Soren—laying in a puddle of his own blood, surrounded by what looked like remnants of the cookie jar.

Mason smiled grimly. Chances were only Jolina waited for him in the dark, but she wasn't to be trifled with and had accurate aim, he recalled.

The trail of debris and destruction led Mason to the dining room, where the air was still thick with the acrid smell of recently fired gunpowder. Crouching low, the gun in his right hand ready to fire, he turned on his flashlight for a quick look. He'd half expected to draw fire, but Jolina didn't give her position away.

Slowly, carefully, every crunch freezing him, he made his way between the broken bodies of porcelain cows, glad that he'd pulled on not just his pants, but his boots as well.

When he swept into the living room, he had his gun ready in front of him and the lit flashlight in his raised left hand, far over his head. Its high intensity beam swung in an arc, covering much of the darkened space. But Jolina wasn't fooled, or blinded. In the time it took for the white light to finish its arc and die, she shot twice, missing Mason by a wide margin, but herding him into the room nonetheless. "Move and I shoot Soren," she yelled, effectively freezing Mason in his tracks.

"No, she—"

A bullet tore into the couch with a muted thump.

In his corner, on his haunches and shielded by a spindly, antique table, Mason cursed silently. He'd had his chance to shoot her, or rather return fire in the direction of the muzzle flash he'd seen, and he hadn't taken it. Now he was without cover. She would see him as soon as he moved—the human eye was very good at detecting motion, even in the dark—and he had no real idea where she was. He was as likely to spot Soren crawling in the dim light spilling in through the louvered windows as he was to come across Jolina changing positions.

"Stay where you are, Soren."

"Yes, stay where you are, Soren," Jolina parroted from somewhere near the arched doorway that led into the front corridor.

Mason cursed. She'd moved, unwilling to let Mason pick her off, no doubt. Unlike Mason, who worried about shooting Soren by accident, he didn't think she had such qualms.

"Drop the gun. Drop it," Jolina hissed from somewhere near the arched doorway. "I will shoot you."

Mason swore. Unless she moved and gave away her position, he had no target. Out of the corner of his eye, he thought he caught movement behind the couch. He shook his head, hoping to God that Soren would get the message, and lowered his weapon.

"That's it," Jolina said. "Put the gun down. Do you wish to die, Mr. Ward?"

"Not today," Mason grumbled. He had to reach to place his gun away from the spilled lilies and the potting soil. Slowly, he straightened to his full height, raised his chin and gave the gun a gentle kick. It slid across the hardwood floor, out of sight and under the couch.

Jolina moved out of the shadows of the hallway. Her gun was aimed squarely at Mason's chest. A smile contorted her features. "Very good. At least one of you boys does as he's told."

In the murky twilight, Jolina kept an eye on Mason. "I will shoot him," she called out. "I will count to five, and I will shoot him. One."

"Stay where you are, Soren. Don't move."

"Two. You do wish to die, Mr. Ward, don't you?"

"Mason."

"Yes, Mason. How could I forget?" Her eyes gleamed brightly.

Mason's cold hard look lost most of its cutting intensity in the adverse illumination or lack thereof.

"He's a good lay, isn't he?" She smiled. "But he's not worth this. Three."

Mason had to give her credit. Her eyes didn't stray. The gun didn't waver.

"I tire of this, Soren." She lowered her gun hand, readjusted her aim and fired. "Four."

The bullet tore through Mason's left thigh, shredding flesh

and muscle, bouncing off the bone. Groaning and cursing, Mason collapsed and clutched his leg. Blood pulsed out of the wound and seeped between his fingers.

"What happened to five?" Soren jumped up from behind the couch, Mason's gun in hand. Unlike Jolina's, his aim wasn't steady, and his eyes were on Mason, not his target. He was bleeding from a multitude of small cuts on his hands and across his bare arms and shoulders. His eyes were bright with defiance and worry.

"I'm a girl. I changed my mind." Jolina raised her gun and stepped closer to Mason. Her next bullet would tear through his chest. "Drop it, Soren."

"I don't think so."

It was a classic stand-off. Her gun was on Mason. Soren's gun was on her. Both of them saw just enough to make out their target.

"I will shoot him."

"Go ahead. He's a bossy prick. Just like my father."

"You're spoiled, selfish, immature, irresponsible, Soren, but I never thought you were stupid enough to rat me out to the feds. What the fuck were you thinking?"

"Drop the gun, Jolina."

"Or what? You'll shoot me? You don't have the guts, Soren. You've never shot anyone before. Look at him. Look at him." She pointed with her gun to the blood pooling under Mason's leg. "Can you do that to a person? To me?"

"You're right." Soren lowered his gun. What he couldn't see clearly in the dusk—blood welling out of Mason's leg and over the hands he had pressed to his wound—his imagination filled in for him in vivid color. He swallowed the panic in his throat and forced his concentration on the woman he'd once cherished. "I am spoiled and selfish. And, God knows, I could use a drink."

"Oh, baby." She smiled, and her eyes softened. "Don't look." She raised her gun to readjust her aim, but the shot that rang out wasn't hers and the bullet that killed wasn't driven through Mason's brain.

"But I have killed before," Soren croaked. He hadn't realized he had stopped breathing. He sucked in a heaving breath, exhaled slowly and peered over the back of the couch to where Jolina had crumpled, her unseeing eyes staring at the upended peace lilies. "Fuck."

"You okay?"

Mason's low voice brought Soren out of his shock. He dropped the gun, limped around the couch and fell to his knees in front of Mason.

Soren's green eyes swept over Mason's bloody hands as they applied pressure to his leg, then up to Mason's eyes. Mason's face was ashen, his lips pale, but his eyes were calm and his voice still commanding. "Call 911. Call my mom. Get me some towels."

"You are a bossy prick."

Mason managed a grin, but pain was beginning to etch lines in his face. "If you let me die, my ghost will haunt you forever."

"Fuck that." Soren scrambled to his feet, groaned, and disappeared him into the kitchen as fast as his protesting hip would allow. He yelled for George and yanked the decorative cow towels off the oven's handlebar. He doubted she would care.

Soren fell to his knees again next to Mason's prone body, pressing the folded towels over the copiously bleeding wound, applying pressure.

"I've killed twice now to protect you," he said, his voice insistent. "I think Kaoru needs a refund. I've done my own protecting," he joked. "Mason?"

Mason's eyes were closed, his face set in a grimace. His hand, slick with blood, came up, blindly reaching for Soren. "You did good, kid," he whispered. "Promise me," he started, his voice failing.

"Anything."

"Don't go. Wait for me," he breathed.

Soren panicked, but a gentle hand brushed his shoulder and his eyes snapped up to George's face. She nodded. "Let me," she said.

Soren scooted over and cradled Mason's head in his lap, cringing at the sight of Mason's blood on his hands and now in Mason's hair. In the light of the green Coleman lantern she'd brought with her, Soren watched George wring the towel around Mason's leg then heard her speak into her cell phone without comprehending what she said or with whom she was talking.

He looked down at Mason's still face and then the hand that covered his on Mason's chest. Dazed, he followed the hand and arm up to George's eyes. When had she stopped talking on the phone?

"Talk to him, honey," she said, her voice strong, but her eyes glistening with unshed tears.

Soren blinked, swallowed, and nodded. What should he say? He'd had sex with Mason. He'd killed for Mason, but he hardly knew the man. He leaned over the bleeding body and his lips brushed Mason's ear. "I won't go," he promised.

33

Soren remained true to his word. He stayed where he was, sitting cross-legged on the littered living room floor, his back to the splintered door jamb, Mason's head in his lap.

George snagged a throw off the couch and draped it around Soren's bare shoulders, then hurried into the kitchen for more towels. On her way back she snatched a blanket from the toppled armchair and covered Mason with it.

"He'll be okay," she whispered, applying pressure to his wound. "He'll be okay." Her fingers shook as she checked his right wrist for his pulse. She left a smear of bright red blood behind.

He was bleeding to death, Soren thought. He saw the color

of the oxygen-rich blood seeping into the towel when George released the tourniquet every so often. He could feel Mason's rapid pulse in the palm of the hand that was cradling the dark head. Most of all, though, he felt it in the weakening hold Mason had on his other hand. The man was everything strong and steadfast, but his strength bled out of him with every beat of his heart.

"I'm sorry," Soren mumbled hoarsely, pushing the words past the panic welling up in his throat. He thought he felt Mason squeeze his hand before the injured man lost his tenuous hold on consciousness. Soren made a low noise in the back of his throat where panic and love were choking him. He didn't know if the words made it past his lips, but they repeated themselves over and over again inside his brain. Oh God, please. I'm sorry. I'm sorry, sorry.

He was only peripherally aware of the time that passed or George's anguish at seeing her son bleeding in his arms. Then people started showing up. Stoney. Two patrol cars, alerted by George's call to her station. Kaoru and his small team of federal agents. The ambulance was lagging behind, though. It had to fight its way through flooded streets clogged with fallen banana trees, parts of tin roofs and other windblown debris.

Timoteo was dragged from his closet. Eleoterio wasn't dead, but would probably wish for death with the headache he was going to suffer. He remained unconscious, but received handcuffs nonetheless. Jolina's dead body was covered.

Soren barely registered the coming and going until the ambulance arrived and paramedics swarmed over Mason. Suddenly he found himself being shoved out of the way, looking down at Mason's prone body. He was too dazed to keep up with the medical exchange, but recognized the urgency. He stepped to the side.

"Soren, honey." George materialized at his side and put her arms around him, clinging to him for her comfort as much as his. Her men's pajamas were stained with Mason's blood. She was as pale as her son, her smile didn't quite reach her eyes, but the comfort she offered was genuine. "Let's get you cleaned up a bit," she said and tried to lead him away.

But Kaoru shook his head at her before addressing Soren, "You okay?"

"Does he look okay?" Soren figured he had to look very much like a man who'd just survived the worst day of his life. His pale skin did nothing to hide a multitude of bruises. Scratches, cuts and the gash on his forearm were oozing blood, which mingled with Mason's. His sweatpants were stained with it. His bare feet were splattered with it. He was exhausted and worn. He felt numb. But past the numbness lay anger.

"I'm fucking great," he spat at Kaoru. "No thanks to you."

Kaoru took a surprised step back. "I—"

"God damn you." Soren shook off the motherly arm of support. His fists balled at his sides. There was enough heat in his voice that George felt compelled to step between the two men, a hand on Soren's chest.

"He called you hours ago. You should have been here."

"I trusted Mason's judgment," Kaoru snapped.

"His judgment?" Stoney stalked in from the hallway. Heads turned and followed his raised voice. "His judgment," he growled, "was compromised by all the information you conveniently forgot to fork over." His dark eyes flashed. "He thought he was taking in a drunk, no offense, Soren, not attracting terrorists. Or that slime Buchanan."

Soren noticed Stoney didn't apologize for his last comment.

"Oh, I get it," Kaoru sneered. "You're trying to pin this on me. News flash, your brother—"

"Don't finish that," Soren warned.

"That's quite enough," George injected, before tempers and testosterone got carried away. She leveled the men with a look that would have made Mason proud. "I won't have this. Not now."

Her calm was remarkable, but the eyes she turned on her firstborn were large and pleading and filled with tears.

"Please ride in the ambulance with your brother," she said quietly.

The men turned to see the paramedics wheel Mason away.

Soren's heart lurched as his eyes swept over the blood left behind, the smear of it across the hardwood floor. A ruined towel, once sterile gauze wrappers and plastic packaging the paramedics had discarded lay next to the peace lilies someone had righted.

He looked up in time to see Stoney trot after the paramedics and started to follow, when his right leg gave out. Pain, acute, demanding, white hot, shot across his hip and pelvis, lodged in his lower spine and traveled like a lightning strike into his thigh.

He would have crashed on his knee, was in fact already bracing for the jarring agony, but George and Kaoru caught him.

"Whoa," Kaoru said.

"Soren, honey?"

"Let's get him to the hospital."

Soren thought that sounded like a wonderful idea. He wanted to lie down. He wanted to sleep. He wanted to get blissfully drugged. Not necessarily in that order, though. Hell, he'd forgo the sleep, if they provided him with some good drugs. The thought of pain relief and oblivion was enough to make him smile as he hobbled between Kaoru and George to the patrol car that was to follow the ambulance, which had already left.

George misread his smile. "I don't think they'll let you share a room," she whispered, her voice gentle. She helped Soren into the backseat where he could stretch out.

All at once Soren felt sick to his stomach. Mason's blood was still warm on his hand and here his thoughts were on drugs again. Hell of a way to redeem himself. He cleared his throat and darted a look at George.

"He'll be okay," he breathed, more question than statement.

"Yes." She straightened, breathed deeply—past the tears and fear—nodded. "Yes, he'll be okay."

34

In the hospital, Soren learned that he'd overestimated the extent of his aches and pains. There were no drugs for him; at least none of the kind he'd been hoping for and the hospital's bland, low-dose painkillers just didn't do it for him. He thought he showed remarkable restraint faced with such grim realities and the endless questions by doctors, nurses, federal agents and police officers. His own questions—Where was Mason? How was he? What were they doing to him?—would have remained largely unanswered if not for Stoney, who fled the family-members-only ICU waiting room every so often to keep Soren informed.

The older twin's last, clipped report, "Bullet took a chunk

of bone out, nicked the artery. Nothing they couldn't fix," went a long way to alleviate Soren's worries. But it wasn't until George's gentle insistence that he get some sleep that Soren allowed himself a reprieve, only to wake up what seemed like minutes later.

"Yo." Stoney lounged on the empty bed next to Soren's, propped up with pillows, shoes kicked off, a soda can in his hands. He took his eyes off the sportscaster on TV and swept them over Soren. They lingered over the bag with crushed ice resting on Soren's right hip. "You doing okay?"

Soren raked a hand through his hair and groaned. "You got anything better than aspirin on you?"

Stoney shook his head and returned his eyes to the TV screen. He looked tired, but he'd lost the pinched, waiting-for-the-worst expression he'd worn earlier.

"How's Mason?"

"He woke up for a minute. He wasn't happy." A smile stole over Stoney's face. "He'll love it in here. He'll grouse about the food, but he'll love the attention. He'll be back on the Sprite in no time."

"I'm sorry."

Stoney nodded, turned off the TV and swung his long legs over the edge of the bed to sit facing Soren. "Listen, I'm sure Kaoru's motives for, uh, handing you over to Mason weren't exactly kosher, but Mason's a grown man. He knew what the hell he was doing. Things just ... stuff happens. Don't apologize." He winked. "I would have shot first, asked questions later, but he's so squeamish when it comes to other people's blood."

Soren nodded. He didn't think for a minute it was that easy for the older twin, but he appreciated Stoney's attempt to ease his mind. "I want to see Mason."

Soren climbed awkwardly out of bed. His body protested with sore muscles and an uncooperative hip. For a brief moment, he considered taking a hot shower that would loosen tense, cramped, tight muscles and restore flexibility to his hip, but his desire to see Mason overrode his discomfort.

He wished for socks, though. His toes were freezing on the

chilled linoleum floor he limped across to get to the door of his room. The hospital gown didn't do much for him either. The problem with hospital gowns wasn't so much that they left the wearer exposed, but that they weren't comfortable or warm enough to do a proper job with the parts of the body they did cover. Stoney's aborted snort made him turn at the door.

"Whoa. You got freckles everywhere," Mason's twin announced, gesturing with his soda in the general direction of Soren's backside. Color stained his cheeks.

"So?"

Stoney threw up his hands. "Let's get you a robe or a wheelchair or something."

"Okay." Soren pulled open the door.

Stoney jumped off the bed, rammed his feet into his shoes and dashed after him.

"This is a Swedish thing, isn't it?" Stoney grumbled as he walked next to the redhead to the nurse's station.

Soren just smirked at him as he concentrated on turning his hobble into a walk. He was so focused on setting one foot in front of the other to work the stiffness from his hip that he didn't notice the embarrassed cop that followed them from his room. Or the man waiting at the nurse's station.

"Buchanan," Stoney snarled.

Soren's head jerked up. His father was the last person he'd expected to run into.

"Officer Ward."

"Listen, Buchanan, I don't think this is—"

"Why don't you just stay out of this? I have things to discuss with my son."

Stoney shook his head. "No. I don't think so."

"It's okay," Soren injected. He had a few things to say to his father. But first he leaned against the nurse's station, smiled his most charming smile and asked for a bathrobe, hoping his voice wouldn't give away how unsettling his father's presence was. How could that man still have a hold on him after all he'd done?

"In your room," James suggested impatiently.

Behind James's back, Stoney shook his head. He had his arms crossed over his chest—his bulging biceps testing the stretch of his shirtsleeve.

"Here's fine. I don't expect this will take very long," Soren countered.

James's lips flattened against his teeth. "You disappoint me. And you know how much I hate disappointments. It upsets me."

Soren rolled his eyes. He knew what this little visit was all about: damage control. His father had to reassert his authority. He knew damn well he'd been knocked off his power-pedestal, and he had to reestablish his dominance. Only this time his son wasn't going to heel with his tail tucked between his legs. Soren had a moment of gleeful anticipation, then said, "I'm not coming home. We're through."

James grabbed Soren's elbow and gave his son a shake. "You are coming home with me. Whatever you told that fed, I do not care, but you are coming home with me."

"Yo, hands off, Buchanan."

James whirled. "Stay out of this. You and that fag brother of yours put—"

"What did you just say?" Soren asked in disbelief.

"Oh, you heard me," James snapped, turning to face his son again. "Enough of this. You are coming home with me now."

Soren took a step back. His green eyes flashed defiance. "If I'm going home with anyone it's that fag brother of his."

James delivered his backhand with the same cold accuracy he used in dealing with his clients. Soren staggered. But he'd expected the blow, he retaliated before Stoney or the security detail could react. His fist caught his father under the chin, driving his teeth into a soft upper lip. James, eyes wide with disbelief, stumbled into the nurse's station, blood dripping from his mouth.

"Don't you dare touch me again," Soren spat. "We're through," he reiterated. He turned and stalked off towards the elevator, hospital gown gaping behind him.

Stoney lingered, looking smug. "Didn't see that one coming, huh? I suggest you take his advice."

James pulled a handkerchief from his breast pocket and dabbed his split lip. "This is not over yet."

Stoney shrugged, snatched the bathrobe from a bewildered looking nurse and hurried after Soren. "Yo, wait up."

In the elevator, Soren sank against the mirrored paneling and shook out his wrist. He flexed his fingers and scowled at his reddened knuckles. "I am so fucked," he announced to no one in particular.

"I think you did pretty good."

Soren raised his eyes from the floor and looked at Stoney. "I just made an enemy I can't afford." Without his father's support and credit cards, Soren was penniless. He had no place to stay. No job. The only thing he owned free and clear was his unreliable, hopelessly rusted Jeep, but unless he planned on sleeping in his Jeep....

Stoney shrugged. "Listen, I'll talk with my mom." He winked and a grin split his face. "She likes you. She'll forgive you the destruction of her cow collection."

Soren shook his head and straightened his shoulders. He needed a clear break. He needed independence. He didn't want to live his life the way he used to, taking too many things for granted, not taking the right things for granted. "I appreciate the offer, I need to do this on my own."

"It's just a couch to crash on, not a free lunch. Until you're on your feet." Stoney waggled his brows, amusement brightening his face. "If you thought Mason was bad, just live with my mom for a week."

35

Six weeks later …
Tradewinds was a fun hang-out, serving up alcohol, live music and the occasional embarrassment during karaoke night. On a quiet side street that had never existed on any map, the bar was within walking distance of the Chamorro Village public market, a popular spot for the lunch crowd, that twice a week, on Wednesdays and Fridays, transformed into a lively night market.

Mason heard the fiesta music as he climbed out of his cab. Still a bit stiff-legged, he walked down the empty alley and pushed through the door of Tradewinds into its dimly lit interior. The music was loud, but comfortably so. The salty breeze off the marina swept in through wide open patio doors and mingled with the aroma of spilled beer and sweaty tourists. The crowd was casually dressed and young. The waitresses wore miniskirts and tight tank tops with the Tradewinds logo emblazoned on them.

The man who owned and managed the bar happened to be related in some way to a second or third cousin of Soren's. Thus, he'd been persuaded to hire Soren, a move he hadn't regretted. Mason had taken Soren's word for it. He'd had his reservations about Soren working with alcohol, but the redhead's job skills were somewhat limited and tending bar seemed to agree with him.

A lot had happened since that night all those weeks ago. The Smile hadn't escaped the attention of the law, but had managed to remain a free man without a criminal record. Slick bastard! Eleoterio and Timoteo Miciano were in federal custody. Kaoru, who'd come to the hospital in his capacity as friend once, smartly avoided the subject. Mason figured he would eventually be called upon to testify against the Filipinos in court. He still marveled over the fact that Soren had managed to kill Jolina with one bullet, but he pushed unbidden thoughts of death aside to focus on his reason for skipping out on his hospital stay a few days early.

Soren was behind the bar, mixing a neon-colored drink and shamelessly flirting with a young Japanese woman whose English sounded about as atrocious as Soren's Japanese had to be.

Mason found himself a spot at the bar near the Japanese girl and waited for Soren to notice him. Soren looked good. Relaxed, fit, confident. There was little wonder his tousled red hair and wide smile attracted female attention. His job definitely agreed with him.

He must have sensed a new customer, because his green eyes swung in Mason's direction. His smile widened with recognition. He ambled over.

"Don't I know you?"

His smile was infectious, and Mason found himself grinning back just as happily. "I seem to recall we've met."

"Should you be in here?"

"Oh? You recommend a different bar?"

"Seriously. What about the hospital? You're not done."

"Yes, I am," Mason corrected. He was sick of the hospital, its bland food and his perpetually upbeat therapist who assured him that his leg would be back to one hundred percent in no time. He knew it would; he didn't need her to tell him. He longed for the comfort of the Sprite and the redhead who lived on her now.

On impulse, still under the effects of sedation and in an effort to keep the redhead close, he'd offered the newly independent and homeless Soren the Sprite to live on. Only later had he started thinking of clothing carelessly dropped, dirty dishes in the sink, and a refrigerator filled with junk food and soft drinks. His fear that his once tidy and immaculate Sprite had deteriorated into a messy first-time-on-his-own bachelor pad as much as his longing to be home had him leaving the hospital early. But there was no reason to divulge the former; he had the perfect excuse: it was the twenty-third of October, which also happened to be Soren's twenty-third birthday.

"I wanted to surprise you. Happy birthday."

Soren's wide smile turned into a foolish grin. "Really? Thanks."

Mason nodded. "How about a beer, barkeep?"

Soren cocked his head to the side. "A man your age with a chunk of bone missing should drink milk."

A tall glass of ice-cold milk did actually sound appealing to Mason, but a chilled beer was what he craved. He opened his mouth to place his order when another of the bar patrons pushed a man into him, jarring his healing leg.

"Watch what you're doing, fag," a guy in a flashy Hawaiian shirt shouted over the music. He pushed the subject of his anger again, but the smaller man had nowhere to go, sandwiched between the aggressor and Mason.

Mason was about to intervene when he heard Soren's voice.

"Yo, asshole," Soren called out. "Watch your language in here or fuck off."

That wasn't the mouthy Soren Mason remembered. The young

man behind the bar stood with his shoulders squared and a very calm, albeit cutting stare directed at the troublemaker. There was no mistaking his stance or expression. He wasn't to be trifled with and no one on his bar would be harassed either. He'd changed. Matured. Mason felt hope ignite. Maybe he'd shed his messy habits, too?

"What's it to you?" the man sneered, sizing up Soren. "He your boyfriend?"

"No," Mason injected. His voice easily carried over the music and past the guy's drunken idiocy. "I am."

The bar patrons who overheard the exchange snickered. A few surprised looks were tossed in Soren's direction. Someone whistled. The man caught in the middle blushed a deep crimson up to his blond roots.

Mason might have lost some weight and his pants rode lower on his hips than before his hospital stay, but he was still six foot four. His shoulders were still broad and square, and his stare had lost none of its edge.

The man in the Hawaiian shirt backed down. But the look he sent Soren's way made Mason's hackles rise.

Mason said, "I suggest you leave."

A beefy bouncer's hand fell on the troublemaker's shoulder, backing up Mason's suggestion. They disappeared in the crowd.

Soren's green eyes settled on Mason. "Beer coming right up. What's your pleasure?"

Mason smiled, placed his order and watched Soren work. He admired the view. His hormones took notice, too.

Since his last hospital visit, Soren had allowed someone to trim his hair. Coppery, early-evening stubble covered his cheeks and chin. A leather and hemp choker was roped around his neck, a single green jade bead dangling from it. It was the exact color of his eyes. His long, healthy legs and nice ass were encased in denim that had seen the wash cycle so many times there was barely color left in them.

Self-conscious, Mason brushed a hand over his chin, checking for drool, then shifted to alleviate the pressure forming behind his zipper.

Soren smirked at him. "So?"

Mason raised a brow. Had he missed something? He shook his head to clear his thoughts.

"You're really done with the hospital?"

"Yes."

Mason saw the speculation in Soren's eyes and a smile curved his lips. Yes, they'd dated, if hospital visits (and a few stolen moments in the privacy of the bathroom) could be considered dating, but they hadn't broached the subject of moving in together during all those visits. Hell, Mason hadn't considered the possibility of a live-in lover when he'd given up his apartment to move on his boat, and right now he wondered if two men could share the small space, but he very much wanted for Soren to stay and become a part of his everyday life.

"So?" he imitated Soren, catching his attention. "When are you coming home?"

Soren looked up from mixing a drink.

Mason experienced a stomach-dropping moment of sheer terror when he thought he might be turned down, then Soren's eyes lit up and the corners of his wide mouth stretched into a smile. "I'll be home in a couple of hours."